"I Saw Three
Being advanced so high…..
I saw my realm well-governed
By reason and not by degree
I saw three souls
Set in operation,
Each in his office.
One to command,
And two to serve.
(Queen Elizabeth 1 circa 1590)

The title of this book is taken from a poem written
by Queen Elizabeth 1 in 1590

I SAW THREE SOULS

by

THEODORA CRANE

"I Saw Three Souls"

This is a work of fiction based on facts surrounding the sacking of Tintern Abbey in 1536.

With the exception of the Tudor Monarchy and recognised historical public figures and servants of the time, all characters are fictional.

Any resemblance to events, people living or dead, is purely coincidental.

The title of this book is taken from a poem written by Queen Elizabeth 1 in 1590

ISBN: 9798684824241

Contents

Acknowledgements

My sincere thanks to my dear husband John for his support and encouragement during the writing and preparation of this book.

I Saw Three Souls

Part One
An Act In Time

Chapter One

Riders Through The Night

The road from Chepstow to Tintern twisted and arched its back like a creature of the night, pushing its way through the forest and racing the River Wye.

A rider, head bent forward against the stinging rain, gripped the reins with white knuckles. His horse, wet with the September storm and sweating from his relentless galloping, gleamed as the moonlight streaked from behind a cloud.

His strong legs were tiring and his muscles burned with the strain of finding a safe footing on the slippery road. At times it was little more than a muddy track between the trees, littered with stones and sharp outcrops of rock. The rider's back ached, his only comfort was that he knew the road well and that he had little more than four miles left to travel. Those following, he guessed, would be forced to travel slower than he, tricked by the forest shadows and the gnarled tree roots that tripped even the most practised horsemen.

Finally, the chilling autumn winds blowing up from the Severn Sea gave chase to the storm clouds and the rain ceased. As the rider approached Tintern Abbey the night was still and peace lay over the valley like an invisible blanket.

Abbot Wyche and his twelve choir monks were at evensong when the rider stumbled up the stone steps and threw open the ancient oak door of the church.

The monks gasped and one jumped up shouting out:

"Who dares to disturb the Abbot at his prayers?"

"Fear not!" replied the rider "Tis Jonathan Fairbrother rode all the way from Chepstow with grave news!"

The Abbot, seeming not to have noticed the intrusion neither stirred nor spoke.

1

The other monks were unsure what to do but the look on the rider's face convinced them that the news he carried was urgent and important.

The monk who had risen to his feet now moved towards the rider and drew him aside:

"What is it man? What ails thee?" he whispered, fear making him breathless.

"The King's men are hard at my heels brother!" The rider's eyes burned as he blurted out his message. "Tis King Harry's work and his servant Rowland Lee!"

King Henry V111 had recently appointed Rowland Lee to the post of President of the King's Council in Wales. Under this man a reign of terror had begun and anyone who broke the law or did not obey the wishes of the King was most cruelly punished.

The Abbot appeared at their side.

"I know thy face Fairbrother" he said reassuringly, sensing the man's distress "What urgent matter brings you to our valley this night?"

The rider fell to his knees and kissed the Abbot's ring. Then, looking up at him, he spoke quickly:

"My Lord Abbot you know that it is the King's wish to break all ties with the old religion. He plans to destroy all the monasteries and to take their lands."

The Abbot interrupted him:

"We have heard all these things from our friends from England but…."

"They are on the road as we speak Lord Abbot!" broke in the rider "The King's men will be here by dawn to take all thy wealth and make a ruin of the Abbey. Look to thyselves! Escape with whatever thou canst carry!"

"Escape to where?" answered the Abbot "This is our home and has been the home of Cistercian brothers for 400 years."

He signalled to the monastic servants and told them to bring food and ale for the rider. Another monk went out into the courtyard and led away the rider's horse to find shelter and food for the loyal beast.

One of the monks spoke out "Lord Abbot there is the cross; should we not save the cross?"

The monks lived a simple life with far fewer valuable items than many other religious orders. Their one treasured possession was a golden cross, set with three large rubies, reputed to have once belonged to St. David.

"The cross" he repeated stroking his chin anxiously "Aye indeed the cross must be kept in Wales."

"Let me take it to Neath Abbey for safe keeping and then on to St. David's when it is safe to travel" offered the rider.

"Thy kindness is a credit to thee" said the Abbot resting his hand on the man's shoulder " but if the King's men are on the road then thy life hath been in danger this night and we ask no more of thee. Rest and take food then get thee gone to safety. Our prayers and thanks go with thee."

Having spoken, the Abbot turned and walked towards the small group of monks who now huddled together in the chancel.

The Abbot thought for a moment before speaking again:

"Brothers be of courage for this night may bring great danger to our order." He looked towards one of the monks, a frail man with bright blue eyes and a young face.

"Brother Talbot thy home is not far from here I believe."

"T'other side of the forest" replied the young monk.

"Then methinks thou knowest the land better than any of our brothers." he went on.

"'Tis true my Lord I have lived in these parts all my life."

"Then this night I must entrust to thee the safe-keeping of The David Cross." The monks looked on in silence as the Abbot spoke calmly but with palpable urgency.

"Brother Luke prepare food for Brother Talbot I prithee, Brother Samuel fetch him a warm cloak and jerkin for the journey."

"Lord Abbot it will take our brother days to reach Neath

and the night is black with storm clouds!" pleaded one of the brothers.

"Fear not for me" Brother Talbot reassured him "I shall rest the night at my home farm."

"It is a long and arduous road Brother," said the Abbot looking deep into the monk's young eyes "but I fear there is little choice if we are to get the cross to safety."

The monks began to scurry around getting everything ready for Brother Talbot to make his escape into the night.

Within an hour a small cart pulled by an unsteady pony was standing by to carry Brother Talbot out of the Wye Valley and cross-country to Neath Abbey.

"We know not what the future holds," said the Abbot solemnly as they prepared to bid farewell to Brother Talbot "but we trust in God and in each other. Take the cross with thee and with the Lord's help it will stay in our native land."

He stretched out his hand and passed the cross, wrapped in a purple velvet cloth, to the young monk. Silently the monk accepted the cross and slipped it inside his jerkin where it lay against his heart.

"God be with all of thee!" shouted Brother Talbot and he jerked the pony into movement. Slowly the animal pulled the cart up the hill and away from the Abbey. Brother Talbot kept his eyes forward, afraid to look back lest his emotions overcame him and he did not have the courage to go on.

When at last he reached the turning, which would take him out of sight of the Abbey, he let himself glance over his shoulder for a few seconds. He shuddered as the wind blew through the outstretched arms of the forest and across the ink black river. The Abbey stood alone in the valley, defiant but helpless.

Through the night echoed the clatter of horses' hooves as the King's men pressed on towards their destination.

On another road a young monk urged on a nervous pony whose every step took him further away from one danger and into   another.

Chapter Two

The Deed Is Done

3rd September 1536. Dawn came with a cruel light, which burned across the horizon and streaked the Welsh coastline with uneven slashes of colour. The sheltered Wye valley trembled as the King's men thundered towards Tintern Abbey. The chattering waves licked the riverbank nervously as the monks knelt in prayer and waited.

They arrived quietly; some thirty men-at-arms including boys as young as twelve. After the frantic ride through the night their leader, an experienced soldier, decided to let the men rest once the Abbey was in sight. With the first morning light they approached the Abbey and were glad to dismount.

The surrender of the monastery was swift and surprisingly little resistance took place. There were no armed men to fight for the religious order, although many staunch Catholic families remained in Wales. Perhaps, like their counterparts in England, the gentry were prepared to bow to the will of the King and profit themselves from the sale of the confiscated land.

There was some talk with Abbot Wyche and then the business began.

The silver, plate and meagre ornaments were catalogued, weighed and loaded into sacks to be taken to the King's treasury. The monks kept out of the way unless they were given orders, which they obeyed immediately. Their hearts were filled with anger and fear, but they remained passive, as the Abbot had instructed.

The stripping of the Abbey's wealth was not enough; the King wanted the lands (which he planned to sell to fill the royal coffers) and he cared not that the buildings were left in ruins. The men spent many hours taking the lead from the Abbey roof and carefully loading it to be sold. When they became tired and full of ale, they grew loud and violent, smashing the glass windows with gusto and jeering as the fabric of the Abbey gave in to the will of the King.

"Food for the King's men!" bawled the Captain, his eyes taking in every inch of the chancel as he spoke.

The monks worked uneasily as the men-at-arms clattered from one part of the abbey to another. The soldiers were laughing amongst themselves, kicking the stone floor with cruel boots like animals pawing the ground, nervous and impatient.

"I hear these monks have a fine old time of it with the drabs from the village" joked one, winking his eye and twitching visibly.

The monastic servants continued to bring in food silently and laid out the wooden table in the refectory with platters of vegetables and black bread.

"Harken I say, methinks the Abbot doth have a fine time with the drabs, so fine he hath caught the French Pox!" the soldier spoke louder until he had caught the eye of a young man whose face could not hide the indignation in his heart. Now he had drawn the bait he was ready for the kill:

"I hear the Abbot and his monkeys here do say their prayers so fast that they muddle their Latin and their Welsh till 'tis all a jumble of nonsense!" he was standing now. The soldier was older than the rest and his body had the swagger of a bully. Holding the servant's eyes with a piercing gaze, he walked towards him menacingly.

Like a hunted creature the man looked anxiously for a means of escape as the soldier bore down upon him. His eyes burned with anger but he knew that to respond could be disastrous for them all. The old man was so close now that his prey could smell the soldier's rancid breath and stinking body.

The soldier leaned further and his face was monstrous. He whispered now:

"I hear that the monks make nonsense of their vespers so that they can be about their work." He moved back and laughed hideously at the terrified young man. "So that they can be loosening the stays of young wenches and rubbing their pillicocks against their fair thighs!"

As the soldier spoke his fist lunged out and grabbed at the servant's genitals. The force with which he pulled and twisted the man's flesh drew a scream of pain, which echoed through the ancient walls of the Abbey.

"On thy knees!" the soldier spat out, his face now sweating so much that drops were running down from his forehead to his clenched jaw. The servant obeyed.

A dozen or so soldiers watched the scene. They knew their fellow soldier and of what he was capable. They were party to it all until now.

"Leave the man!" ventured one nervously "He's little more than a boy! Eat thy bread and send him in search of wine."

The soldier did not take his eyes from the young man's face. He repeated:

"On thy knees for the King's soldier hath a little job for thee!" As he spoke he fumbled with the laces on his breeches, which strained with excitement.

The servant began to pray: "Virgin Mary.....sweet Jesu ...." He grunted with fear as the soldier grabbed his head and pulled it toward his groin.

Jonathan Fairbrother had waited long enough. From behind the oak door of the refectory he made his entrance noisily, shouting welcome to the soldiers and waving his arms as if he were drunk. It was all the distraction that was needed. As the soldiers turned in surprise the young man darted across the floor, his knees already bleeding where he had scraped the stones in his escape.

The others welcomed this intervention, the tension disappeared and with relief they accepted Jonathan Fairbrother who brought with him a jug of ale. The old soldier bit into his lip and fastened his breeches before he turned to face Fairbrother. When he did he saw a drunken fool who was trying to win favour with his friends and probably did not know what he had interrupted. The soldier wiped his forehead with his jerkin sleeve and made his way to the table. He was hungry and thirsty. He could wait. The servant could wait. This was an experienced soldier who could take his time and await his chance. No one got the better of the King's men – not this one anyway.

Among the King's men was William Glover, aged 15, a strong boy with a blaze of curly, auburn hair.

"Thou wilt not fail with those curls!" joked a fellow soldier "Why 'tis hair like the King's own!"

"A golden headed Tudor alright!" shouted another and they teased the boy because his colouring was so striking. He was also quick-witted and clever and he was learning fast. He watched and listened, so that when he had a minute in the refectory he noticed places set for the Abbot and twelve monks.

"Forgive me Lord Abbot" he boldly questioned "but how many choir monks be there at the Abbey?"

"Why there are twelve" answered the Abbot.

The Captain turned to William Glover and gaped at the boy's forward ways: "Go on boy!" he encouraged.

"Methinks I need to be better schooled for I have counted only eleven choir monks this day" went on young Glover.

The Abbot made an excuse about a monk being ill and going home.

"And when was this?" demanded the Captain.

"Just ahead of thee I believe." answered the Abbot.

William Glover recognised unease in the old man's face and decided to continue with his thoughts:

"My family are from Devon, Lord Abbot but I have cousins in Pembroke"

"That is your good fortune sir." replied the Abbot maintaining his calm.

"Aye indeed sir," said William Glover "and there is a tale in those parts about a precious cross."

8

"Is there indeed?" answered the Abbot, his voice beginning to show his anxiety.

The Captain looked on in amazement.

"A golden cross called The David Cross. It is said to be kept in this Abbey, although there's many a man in the west as thinks the cross should be at St. David's in Pembroke."

"And there's many a man here" butted in the Captain "as thinks the cross should be in King Henry's pocket!"

Once William Glover had planted the seed in his Captain's head the truth was soon discovered. The thirty-five monastic servants were lined up, questioned and finally threatened until the truth about Brother Talbot's escape was revealed.

It was easy work for the King's men when rumours of cruelty and murder had been spread abroad before they had even arrived. Since the soldiers had been at the Abbey they had used freely the violence that accompanied their power. There was little need for more.

It was easy work for William Glover too, who had watched and waited and now would reap the rewards.

The Captain barked at his men:

"I need three men to ride with Will Glover" he strode around the Abbey gardens kicking at the neatly planted vegetables that the monks relied on for food. "I need three men who will follow Will and take his orders, for he hath more sense than the rest of thee all told!"

William Glover stood listening, knowing that he had earned his chance to prove himself and gain promotion.

"Us'll not take orders from a young hot-head like Will!" grumbled one soldier. It was the old soldier whose lust had been thwarted in the refectory. He was tired of Tintern now and wanted to be back on the road to England. The burning and breaking had been exciting but enough was enough. Also he had hidden in his pocket a small silver box found in the rubble and he intended to make his own little profit from the visit.

The Captain's response was fast and forceful. His arm, gloved in toughened leather swung down at the soldier and smacked across his face. The man reeled, fell and then rolled on the muddy ground. Blood streamed from his mouth and he spat out a gory mess of tooth and flesh as he tried to stand.

"Well i'faith there's my first volunteer!" grinned the Captain "Now who else will join him for the ride?"

The message was clear and two others grunted in compliance, skulking away to join Will Glover who was already waiting with fresh horses.

"Pray do not frown so!" joked Will as the three mounted their steeds "I have made sure thy saddle bags are packed with pies and ale for the journey."

The men did not reply. The old soldier with the bloody mouth spat again on to the floor.

"As for thee" Will said softly, holding the man with his eyes "thy mouth will soon heal when we sell that silver box in thy pocket!"

The man's swollen mouth gaped in fear and surprise when he heard Will's words. He could not have spoken in reply had he wished to, but Will left him no time anyway.

"Trust in me boys," he shouted, "We shall find this runaway monk and his golden cross! Follow me closely for the road to Neath Abbey is a hard one!"

"How doth he know that?" whispered one soldier to another "For he hath come like us to this foreign place."

"I know not," replied his friend "I know nothing of this red-haired jackanapes!"

"And little dost thou need to know" called out Will, just to let them know that he was listening and intended to miss nothing.

He did not want to make them more resentful, however, so he smiled and winked at them:

"We shall do well I promise thee. Neath Abbey hath more riches than this dry place and the King will look kindly on those who bring him The David Cross.

Jonathan Fairbrother watched them leave the Abbey and was relieved to see the old soldier was one of the party. It was time for him to leave Tintern, he had done all he could to warn the monks and had in some small part helped them.

They would all be leaving soon. All but one young servant. His broken body had been dragged from the long reeds at the edge of the river. He lay white against the riverbank shocked and bleached in death. The long slim legs were striped with blood and slashed in the determined brutality of the attack. His murderer kept his eyes on the ground and his head hung low, nursing his bruised mouth. He had taken his revenge and was glad to be leaving before the deed was discovered.

When Jonathan Fairbrother heard of the murder some days later his brain burned for revenge.

"And this in the name of the King!" he muttered. "It is a crime against man and God!"

Will Glover was a splendid sight as he galloped out of the valley. He swung round on his horse, a grey with a magnificent mane and wild, fiery eyes. With a face fired by excitement and enthusiasm, his every word and movement inspired confidence in those around him. Somehow, within a mile or two, his men had settled and without realising it they were loyal and true to their young leader. For William Glover the future was looking good.

Chapter Three

Coming Home

The Talbot Farmhouse was typical of the time. It was built to the cruck design with curved timbers that met at the centre to support the walls and roof. The walls were mostly clay and straw, although animal hair, dung and small stones were mixed in to strengthen the sides. The roof was thatched and smoke curled out from a hole in its centre.

Young Master Talbot and his wife worked the fertile lower lands of the valley. They grew wheat, turnips, onions and swede and, in good years, beans and peas. They had a few sheep, which grazed on the higher ground and kept goats for milk and cheese.

This year's harvest had been good and Master Talbot was sitting contentedly with his wife and their new baby. The goats munched their feed quietly in the corner of the farmhouse living room and the open fire spluttered in the gloomy light.

They heard the farm gate swing open and footsteps running towards the house.

"Master Talbot! Master Talbot come quick!" a voice cried out.

The farmer jumped to his feet and pulled open the farmhouse door.

"Prithee man what's amiss?" he called out to his neighbour.

"An accident Talbot, down on the Neath road and 'tis thy brother!"

"Nay, my brother is over yon in Tintern Abbey" argued Master Talbot, grabbing his thick woollen coat from behind the farmhouse door.

Mistress Talbot emerged, her baby now crying and red-faced.

The neighbour looked past Master Talbot and wrung his hands anxiously:

"Oh mistress 'tis a terrible commotion on the Neath Road, a young man in a cart hath gone down in the ditch and is sorely hurt. His pony was screaming with its leg caught in a trap."

"Lord have mercy!" cried the young woman, crossing herself and holding her child tighter to her chest.

"Get thee back to the house!" shouted her husband "This is not for thee and the child!"

He hurried after his neighbour, frantically wondering why his younger brother might be out in a cart in the dark of night. He wondered desperately if they could possibly be mistaken.

The neighbour said no more for he knew well the two Talbot brothers. One had stayed to farm the land and the other had left his home to become a monk some eight or nine years ago.

Brother Talbot looked up into his brother's face and smiled. At a glance Master Talbot recognised the pale gaunt features of his younger brother and realised that he was seriously injured.

Two farm labourers from another village were fast approaching with a litter and a thick homespun blanket.

"Gentle with him" urged Master Talbot as his brother was lifted onto the litter and secured with strips of loosely woven cloth.

They left the remains of the broken cart in the ditch as a warning to others travelling that treacherous road and began discussing what to do with the body of the horse that was now mercifully out of his misery.

Master Talbot left his neighbours to this sad task and with help carried his brother home.

Mistress Talbot was waiting by the gate and now ran into the house to prepare a bed for the injured man. There were but two rooms in the farmhouse, a living room and a bedroom. She put fresh straw on the floor and covered it with a soft hay mattress. On this bed she lay a cloth roughly woven by her own hands some months before.

She cried out when she recognised her brother-in-law and saw the deep gashes on his bruised body.

"The horse strayed........" Brother Talbot began "I could not hold him in the wind and rain.......... animal trap left by the ditch........couldn't keep him steady."

"Hush!" breathed Mistress Talbot "Thou art safely home sweet brother."

She supported him with her strong young arms as he sipped from the cup she offered. In the cup was bragot, a brew of mulled ale, sweetened and spiced, which she had prepared for the Harvest Supper. It touched his lips and slipped down his throat like warm honey, soothing and healing as he swallowed. Exhaustion overcame him and he was blessed with a dreamless sleep that lasted well into the next day.

When Brother Talbot opened his eyes the first thing he saw was a baby sleeping in a rough-hewn wooden cot by his bed. He tried hard to recall the incidents that had brought him home.

He attempted to sit up in bed but the pain in his legs and back made him shout out and brought Mistress Talbot running into the room.

"Good morrow young brother" she said smiling. One look at his grey face told her that he was very ill indeed.

"Where be thy husband, my brother?" asked the young monk, seeming agitated and afraid.

"Rest thyself I shall find him for thee" Mistress Talbot replied, "he hath hardly slept for worry."

She left the room and went outside to call for her husband.

"There's something amiss" she confided as they entered the house "he be awful upset and his colour is bad. Should I send for someone to bleed him?"

"Bless thee wife," said her husband kindly "thou hast nursed him well. Leave us now so that he might talk with me alone. Rest will heal him and if not then thou must get thy herbs and make a poultice for him."

Master Talbot was shocked however when he saw his brother's pallid features. He sat at his brother's side, silently listening to the details of that fatal night. He heard about the King's men heading for the Abbey and how the Abbot had given The David Cross to his brother to carry to Neath Abbey.

"But the men will go on to Neath Abbey too and all the monasteries" Master Talbot interrupted at one point "the cross will not be safe there!"

He said nothing more for the energy was draining fast from his brother who desperately needed time to finish the story.

"The cross was in my jerkin….." beads of sweat formed on the monks fore head as he struggled to speak "you must find it……..wrapped in purple ……lost it when the cart turned………"

Master Talbot bent towards his brother whose voice trailed off into silence. The monk's breathing was shallow now and a small trickle of blood ran from his left ear onto the pallet.

"Bless thee brother how might I help thee? Shall we pray?" offered Master Talbot unprepared for this rapid decline in his brother's condition.

The monk did not speak but raised his eyes to heaven. Master Talbot began to pray quietly but had barely said a few words when a gurgling sound rattled in the monk's throat and his chest jerked several times. Then there was silence. The fixed gaze in the monk's eyes and the stillness of his heart told Master Talbot that his brother was now at peace.

William Glover and his men were making good time when they spotted the overturned cart and freshly dug mound like a grave at the roadside. They stopped and Will jumped from his horse to examine the site.

"Rest thy backs men!" he shouted to the others who gratefully sprawled out on the grass. They poured ale down their throats from leather flasks and broke off chunks of thick, course bread to eat.

The September sunshine burnished the woodland that skirted the road and warmed the aching bodies of the travellers.

Will studied the cart and then looked around for someone who could give him information. A young boy was leading a goat along the road and he cowered when he saw the King's men:

"What's amiss here?" he asked pointing to the cart and noting the fear in the boy's eyes.

The boy looked at the ground and said nothing.

William Glover stood up as tall as he could make himself and yelled again:

"Didst thou not hear me young fool?"

The boy yelled back at Will, a mouthful of angry words that meant nothing to the King's men.

"He be talking Welsh to thee!" called out one of the soldiers and they all began to laugh.

The boy pulled on the rope, which held the goat and ran off into the wood.

Will decided to laugh along with his men. It was a skill, he was learning, to know when to act and when to humour your way out of confrontation. He was mastering that skill.

Master Talbot was watching this incident from the wood. As the boy ran past him he put his finger to his lips lest the child give him away.

William Glover bent down to examine the cart more closely and then viciously kicked it with his foot.

"Is this the monk's cart?" he thought aloud.

"Pray let us go down to the farms and root out these villains!" suggested the oldest of the men-at-arms. "Fire the barns and slaughter a few beast, that should tell us if the monk is hiding out anywhere!" One of the others cheered and shook his fist.

"And if he is not" broke in their leader "and this is nothing to do with The David Cross, then we have lost valuable time."

"Aye lad 'tis true but what jest it would be" the old soldier continued "these country folk can carry no tales back to England so we can do as we please."

Glover sensed the corruption that hung around the man and was repulsed by him.

Then William Glover made the decision that he was to regret for many years to come.

"Nay lads" he spoke with authority "Let us go on to the monastery. My gut tells me that the monks are marvelling at the cross as we speak!" He mounted his horse and his men immediately followed. The road to Neath squelched under the horses' feet as they cantered and churned mud spat at their backs.

When they were gone Master Talbot came out of hiding in the wood. He walked slowly to the cart, his heart heavy with grief for his brother. Tears blurred his vision for a moment but he rubbed them away as he focused on the deep rich mud around one wheel of the cart. The autumn sun played with the shadows and teased the shapes in the drying earth. Something caught his eye. He was right! He glimpsed a thin line of purple sticking out of the mud. Cautiously he looked quickly over his shoulder and then forced his thick fingers into the wet mire. He felt the cloth, now slimy and slippery, under the surface. Then something hard and sharp. When he nervously explored further as best he could, the hard metal cross bit back in answer to his touch. Without looking more closely, he pulled the sodden brown shape out of the ground and pushed it into his pocket. It felt heavy like lead.

Master Talbot remembered nothing of his walk back to the farm or what he said to his wife who waited anxiously for his return.

His next memory was of washing the cross in warm water and of his dear wife's gasp of disbelief as the beauty of the glistening red stones was uncovered.

"This must be our secret" he whispered to her "There is no safe place for this cross while the King's men are roaming the land."

"Pray what shall we do?" she questioned.

"Keep it here at the farm" Master Talbot replied.

"What if they cometh here in search of it?" asked Mistress Talbot.

"I doubt they will" he answered, "but if they do they must hunt for it, for I shall never betray my brother and hand it over to them."

And so it was that The David Cross came to be at Talbot Farm and there it remained secretly hidden for many years.

Part Two
Thirty Years Later

Chapter Four
Talbot Farm

3rd September 1566. Life in England and Wales had moved on. King Henry V111 no longer ruled and in his place was, not the longed-for son Edward, but his daughter Elizabeth.

Elizabeth had survived against the odds and became Queen at only twenty-five years of age. The new queen was a strong Tudor monarch with a desire for peace in her land and an end to religious persecution.

She had the fine expressive face of her mother Anne Boleyn and the auburn tresses of her father. She also had the cunning determination of her long-dead mother and the ruthless will of her deceased father.

In 1566 she was 33 years old and already the burden of kingship weighed heavily on her. In the last few years she had moved from being a prisoner in the Tower to being Queen of a divided nation. Miraculously she had survived smallpox and outwitted those who predicted that she would lose her throne within months of gaining it. Now Parliament was hounding her with two issues: the Queen's marriage and the royal succession. They would harass her for years to come.

Talbot Farm had changed too. The farmhouse now had a chimney and several more rooms built on to the original dwelling. Outhouses had been put up to shelter the goats, chickens and pigs that were now bred on the farm. An orchard had been planted and at this time hung heavy with cider apples and plump pears.

Master Talbot had recently re-married a young woman from Pembrokeshire. His first wife, whom he had loved dearly, died of fever one stifling summer day. She had borne seven children but only one had survived. They had been unlucky, although in these parts over half the children borne died before reaching the age of one year. A bleak winter or a failed crop could wipe out the youngest and the weakest in a whole village.

The only child was a boy, named John, now aged 12 years and he had no memory of his mother. John was small for his age and limped badly. He was quiet and rather spoilt; used to having his own way and indulged by his father. His best friend was a black and white collie, born like him on the farm. Her name was Tess and she was devoted to her master. The dog, however, was also devoted to Bethan who worked in the farm kitchen and saved all the best scraps for Tess. She was bred to be a working dog and she was quick and clever like all the sheep dogs in her family. Tess liked to think she was as fierce and threatening as the other farm dogs, indeed she could be quite alarming to a stranger. Most of the dog's life however was spent at young John Talbot's heels, playing in the fields or sleeping by the open fire.

"Bethan!" called out Mistress Talbot impatiently.

"Anon Mistress Sarah!" answered the young servant; hitching up her long skirts for fear that she might trip on the uneven stone floor.

"Help me fold the linen Bethan for mercy's sake, I am rushed off my poor feet with the housekeeper sick with the ague."

Bethan hurried to help her Mistress who was clearly not used to doing much around the house. She was puffing out her rosy cheeks, struggling with outstretched arms and fast spoiling the fresh linen by dragging it across the rushes on the floor.

"Let me help thee," offered Bethan, taking the job over and sorting it out perfectly in a matter of minutes "take some ease mistress."

Sarah Talbot flopped down on the bed and fanned herself with a small lace kerchief. Her pink childlike face was damp with perspiration and her golden curls were tumbling from under her cap.

"Pray look at the state I am in!" she said breathlessly "I shall suffer for this sure as eggs is eggs!"

Bethan smiled to herself, for she had heard this many times before, usually when her Mistress had to help with work around the farmhouse.

"Can I fetch thee a little ale mistress or some water from the spring?"

"Aye Bethan aye" answered Sarah Talbot "a drop of ale to tempt me lest I faint off."

Bethan carried the linen over her arm and moved out of the Talbot's bedroom. Her mistress called out:

"Just a drop I prithee girl." she hesitated and then went on "Well, fill the cup and sweeten it with a little honey and some cinnamon from my spice box. I needs must look after myself with all this work I am forced to do."

John, listening to this conversation caught Bethan's eye as she passed and smiled:

"'Tis a hard life on the Talbot Farm!" he imitated his step-mother's voice "Sure as eggs is eggs 'tis too hard for me!"

Bethan wanted to laugh but she ignored this rudeness for she could not help but like her new mistress and did not want to make fun of her. Tess jumped up and followed Bethan to the kitchen on the off chance that some tasty morsel might be thrown her way.

Master Talbot approached the house. He recognised the slight figure of Bethan with her long black hair tied at the back of her neck. She was still a child, the daughter of his best farm labourer, but she worked hard and had a sensible head on her shoulders. She was about the same age as John but had led a different life and she was used to looking after others. When the last bout of plague visited the county she was orphaned and her home was now with the Talbots.

"Good morrow Master Talbot" she said as he entered the farmhouse.

"Good morrow Bethan" he replied, "Does all go well with thee?"

"All is well thank'ee Master" she answered. "The mistress is tired from folding linen and I am fetching her some ale."

"Tired from folding linen!" thought Talbot "How can one so young and healthy be tired from folding linen!"

He remembered his first wife and how she had worked alongside him in the fields, planting the orchard, and gathering the crops at harvest. He stopped himself; it was too painful to look back over the years and times had changed. His new wife was young and he must be patient.

He found her sitting in the living room opposite John. Tess, disappointed, had returned from the kitchen and lay at their feet.

"She is like a fine doll" he mused as he looked at her big blue eyes and her soft pink cheeks "maybe she is not suited to a farm like this."

John watched as his father bent down to greet his wife and listened as he inquired about her health and how she was feeling.

"Oh no!" John thought to himself "I pray thee do not ask her that, we shall have the talk of Tenby and Robert Recorde yet again!"

Too late! Mistress Sarah, feeling genuinely sorry for herself began:

"Dear husband thou art the kindest, sweetest man in all the land but I do so miss my home and family." Her blue eyes filled with tears and Master Talbot picked up her small white hand and held it to his lips. "I am not used to the farming ways" she went on "for my father is a merchant as you know and I am used to his fine house in Tenby." Her well-covered frame shook a little as she gave in to her emotions and cried.

"Come, come, my dear" comforted Master Talbot "'Tis only to be expected that thou should miss thy home at first. 'Twill pass and soon thou shalt love these hills and valleys as we do."

"I know not what my mother would say were she to see me working here" she went on, her tears giving way to anger now, "for as you know sir, I am related to Robert Recorde who was physician to King Henry's son Edward and to Queen Mary............."

At this point they all stopped listening and even Tess shut her eyes and her ears.

"And look what happened to Edward!" John wanted to say remembering that the young King had died despite the care of Robert Recorde and all his other physicians.

Thankfully Bethan appeared at that moment with refreshment for them all and some Barabrith for her mistress.

"Oh Bethan thou art a good child!" exclaimed Mistress Talbot and as she relished her food the tears were suddenly all gone.

Chapter Five

A Face From The Past

The search for The David Cross some thirty years before had proved to be a fiasco for William Glover. They found no trace of the monk at Neath Abbey and when the soldiers finally returned to Tintern to rejoin the King's men they were faced with ridicule. The Captain had put his trust in Will and he had let him down. It was a mistake that the Captain would never make again.

"And what think thee of thy men at arms young Glover?" the Captain hurled at him in front of all the company.

Will Glover's face burned with shame to be humiliated in this way. He cleared his throat and answered as confidently as he could:

"Good honest soldiers Captain. They rode well and never shamed the name of the King."

The Captain strode towards Glover and spat full in his face.

"Good honest men be they?" he yelled. He was furious now at the delay this had caused and the fool he felt for letting a youngster take off like that.

"Well Christ preserve me from good honest men for one is thief and the other is a murderer!"

Despite the Captain's authority he had been presented with evidence by the Abbot to show that two of the men who had gone with Glover, were involved in the murder of the young servant at Tintern. The silver box had been found hidden in the refectory and given to the servant to take to the Captain. Before he could do that he was waylaid by the old soldier and his accomplice, who stole it from him. They had then proceeded to beat the young man and commit acts of unspeakable vulgarity on him. The Captain lived in a violent world but this could not be tolerated. He must be seen to maintain power over his men and be ready to discipline them. He gave orders for the two soldiers to be taken to the nearest tree and hung.

"And let it be for all the folk to see!" the Captain shouted as the accused men were dragged away. "Hang them by the River that those who travel the Wye will see them. Then they will know King Henry's justice and be in fear of it!"

William Glover returned home in shame, having felt the bitter sting of humiliation. He was sure that he was right and that the cross was somewhere between Tintern and Neath Abbey, but he had been forbidden to waste any more of the King's time searching for it. He had been held responsible for the conduct of two men that he had neither chosen nor befriended. He had in fact managed to control their bloodlust while they were with him and gained their respect. There were, however, no ears to hear the case of a young inexperienced soldier however brilliant he may be. The Captain had been embarrassed and Glover paid the price!

In the years ahead the story was twisted and enlarged until few could remember exactly what William Glover had done wrong – some said nothing and others whispered murder.

William Glover had continued to serve the King and made a fair living out of it one way or another, although he never gained the promotion he had so desired. He was a survivor and as the monarchy changed so William listened and learnt. He had never forgotten The David Cross, however, and when he decided to quit the service and return home, it was still there nagging at him from the past.

"How different my life would have been;" he thought "Perchance I could have been the most favoured of all the King's men!" William Glover could not hide his bitterness when he thought of the life he might have had; the wealth, the respect and most of all the power.

Driven by this frustration he returned to Tintern Abbey, now a magnificent ivy clad ruin, and the memories still smacked him hard and raged in his soul. From there he rode on to the old Neath road, slowing his horse down to a trot when he reached the wooded area which he thought was the site of the over-turned cart.

There was no sign at all of the mound where someone or something had been buried or of the wooden cart.

"Thinkest thou that these things would still be here?" he asked himself aloud in a mocking whisper.

He stopped, dismounted and thought hard. Though he was now 45 years old his hair still blazed like gold and his mind was sharper than ever. He felt that he was close to the truth and so decided to stay overnight in the nearest inn to the road. He remembered the boy with the goat and how he had run off into the wood. There must be something on the other side of the wood, a village perhaps or a farm.

Leading the horse through the wood, Will marvelled that this at least looked exactly as he had remembered it. The canopy of branches was hung with dying leaves. For years the ancient trees had been bathed in sunshine and caressed by soft breezes blowing up the valley and across the hillside. The sky was white and soft, under bellied like a mushroom with brown furrows.

Deep in the wood was a small community who made their living from the woodland around them. They had built wooden shelters, which covered with animal hides, proved good protection against wind and weather. Wood was collected for fuel and sold in bundles at markets and around the farms. Rabbits were caught and sold on or eaten by the hunters, animal fur and hides cured and fashioned into all manner of items, charcoal burnt and wood planed and chiselled into furniture and household utensils.

The woodlanders were suspicious of strangers.

"Good day to thee" said Glover, smiling to win their confidence.

He was ignored and so tried again.

"Forgive me sirs for approaching thee in this rude manner" he paused and hoped that they were not Welsh speakers.

"What brings thee to these woods stranger?" someone asked.

"I seek shelter for the night…" William began but was quickly interrupted:

"No inns round here for thee, not for ten mile or more." the voice continued.

A man stepped out of the shadows and faced Glover.

"I remember thee" he snarled "Thou art one of the King's men, come here to burn and pillage." The man smiled at William showing blackened stumps where his teeth once had been. "Frightened me on the road there, thou hast forgotten that I suppose?"

Glover could not believe his luck! This was the young boy with the goat!

He smiled with relief "I do indeed remember thee and thy goat" he answered, "and I remember that I did thee no harm nor thy kith and kin!"

The man was still coming forward at Will and his fists were clenched at his side.

William felt for his purse strapped at his waist and quickly took a few coins from it. The man stopped and looked down at the coins now being offered to him.

He spoke quickly, becoming aware of a group of woodmen that had gathered around him. Despite his strong muscular body and experience of combat, the odds were against William and he was tired from his journey. This would be a fight he might lose and William Glover was tired of losing:

"Tell me about the accident on the road that day and who was buried in the grave by the cart there."

No reply.

"Tell me and these coins are for thee."

"Methinks those coins are mine now any way" said the man and several of those around him laughed and repeated his words among themselves.

Quite near to where they were standing was a low hut built partly of branches but closely draped with skins. Across the entrance was a heavy woven cloth blackened by smoke from the fire. This was pulled aside and a woman stepped out. She called across to the men in Welsh and then came forward towards Will Glover.

"I can help thee" she said slowly still moving towards Will.

She was wearing a dark woollen shawl pulled tightly around her body, a skirt that dipped into the puddled woodland floor and a cap, which might once have been grey or even white. Long waves of russet hair spilled from the cap, defying the order it tried to impose. Her skin was smooth and dusky with wood smoke from her fires. The face was challenging and bold, finely chiselled with full-curved eyebrows. Her eyes mocked and flashed, teasing with a strange hue that was between grey and green.

She stretched out her hand to take the coins and as she did so let the shawl fall from her shoulders. The men began to shout and laugh as the woman bared her ample breasts.

"See what I got for thee stranger" she said smiling. Digging one of her heels into the muddy ground she began to move this way and that, swaying her hips. Will tried to take his eyes from her naked chest but her movement was hypnotic. Her skin was brown like leather but her teeth were strong and white. There was an earthy smell about her, but one that was tempered by an aromatic blend of marigold and lavender. It was a pungent, powerful device.

She took his hand and went to place it on her breast but one of the men intervened.

"Get back to thy stews woman!" he called out to her "Dost thou want to bring plague to the forest?"

The spell was broken. The woman curled her lip and snarled at the men in her native tongue. As she went back inside her home William could hear a child crying and he was glad that he had not been tempted to follow her.

Will turned again to face the man and continued, determined to seek the truth:

"I prithee say good sir who lies in that grave, for I am in fear that 'tis a cousin of mine, a monk who I loved dearly."

The men laughed again and Glover stiffened, tired of their mockery.

"'Tis no monk in that grave my man, 'tis a horse that's all." replied the man at last.

Disappointment surged through William's veins and he grudgingly handed the coins to the man.

"The poor beast was caught in a trap" the man went on "but the monk survived."

Will had turned to leave the wood but now he swung round on his heels and his eyes sparked like fire:

"The monk is alive?" he asked, not able to believe that at last his luck was changing.

"Lord no! He lasted but a day. He is buried over at the Talbot Farm," said the man pointing towards the edge of the wood.

Talbot! The name rang in his ears. Brother Talbot was the name of the twelfth choir monk!

"But thou should know the farm if thee truly be a cousin of the monk" said the man, looking aggressive again.

Will did not wait to discuss the matter further. He took more coins from his purse, scattered them on the ground and in an instant he had straddled his horse and was off through the wood and into the field beyond.

William Glover strode up the path leading to the Talbot farmhouse. The autumn sunshine was still powerful; it gilded the harvested fields in a show of defiance against the dying stubble. Roses, which grew wild in the hedgerow by the farm, hung their heads and gave up their sweet fragrance without complaint. As he approached the dwelling, his soldier's boots brushed against crowds of lavender that rustled and shook their dried heads. The combination of lavender and rose made a heady perfume that pleased Will Glover and lingered in his mind. He suddenly thought of the woman in the forest, but quickly pushed that aside. This was a gentle, more subtle fragrance.

He knocked loudly on the door and Tess jumped to her feet barking. Mistress Sarah Talbot was sitting inside with a basket of dried lavender at her side. She was carefully stitching the edge of muslin bags and filling them with grey-blue heads.

"Bethan" she called out "Pray see who knocks at the door!"

Bethan was out of earshot however; feeding the chickens at the back of the house with John. Tess had not been allowed to follow them as she scared the chickens and worried the goats.

The door was banged again and this time the mistress shuffled to her feet and pulled open the door.

She was at her loveliest, the golden curls framing her cherubic features. Her sleepy blue eyes flashed like precious gems when she looked up at her visitor and her perfect white teeth smiled in welcome. It was a face that would stay in his mind.

Tess followed Mistress Talbot to the door. She sensed that the man was a stranger and so began shoving her way between them, barking, sniffing and snapping viciously at Glover's leather boots.

Mistress Sarah bent down to calm the dog saying:

"Forgive me sir, she is usually the meekest of souls. Hush Tess, hush!"

It was not difficult for William Glover to talk his way into the farmhouse. Skilfully Glover established that this was the home of Master Talbot, the brother of the monk who lost his life on the road some years ago. He explained that he was a distant relative of the family travelling in the area and wished to renew his acquaintance with his cousins.

"Pray is your father at home mistress?" enquired William Glover, his grey eyes searching Sarah's startled face.

Standing in the doorway to her home Sarah Talbot was stunned by the presence of this man. Despite his years, William Glover's hair was thickly curled. His skin was unmarked by the pox which scarred so many and also seemed to glow where the summer had tanned his features. The lines around his eyes hinted at the strength and resolve gained from his experiences. As to the colour, Sarah Talbot was not sure. She had taken in so much of his face in the minutes he had held her in conversation, yet the soft hue of his eyes eluded her.

"Mistress…?" William Glover repeated, jolting her from her observations.

"Nay forgive me sir, come in cousin." Sara Talbot stepped back and allowed William Glover to enter her home and her life.

"Master Talbot, my husband" she replied, looking away from him as she corrected that mistake "is on the road from Llantarnam as we speak. He hath business there but I trust he will be home afore night time if thou wouldst rest awhile."

Glover had arrived at the farmhouse driven by his desire to seek out the truth and to be compensated for the past thirty years of indignity fate had dealt him. He was unprepared for Sarah Talbot and the effect she had on his body and mind. He was not a womaniser, though God knows he had taken women in a fleeting loveless way when he needed to. Mayhap he had fathered a few offspring over the years but that was the way of the King's men. Glover's main concern was to keep free of the disease-ridden strumpets that followed the camp and to turn his thoughts away from commitment.

This woman had been like an assault on his senses and his emotions were confused. The lavender filled farmhouse became stifling, the mood unstable.

William Glover regained control. He had the information he was seeking and needed to make a quick exit. Abruptly he was away, his blood coursing and his brain racing. The meeting had raised the most basic of instincts to the surface of his conscious mind. Too many times he had seen men lose control of their bodies in that situation and he had been uncomfortably close to losing his.

Glover was, therefore at his most frustrated and reckless when he made his next acquaintance. It was the woman from the forest picking blackberries at the side of the road. Her grin welcomed his rough embrace. Her hands soiled and stained purple from the fruit, pulled at his curls as he lifted her skirts. His mouth found her breasts and they gave him the pleasure they had promised. She gasped and chuckled deep in her throat as his body spent its passion inside her. When it was over he was emptied of all feeling. She willingly accepted the coins he gave her and without conversation they parted company. Some moments later as he started back on the road, she shouted after him: "There's an inn a mile North". He raised his hand as a gesture of thanks but dare not look back at her. He was glad to be on the road again.

Sarah Talbot went back to her task, but her small girlish fingers trembled too much to sew and her thoughts were in turmoil. She had dreaded a moment like this, since the day her loving father had betrothed her to her equally doting husband.

Also she had been wrong in thinking that her husband was several miles away. He had successfully concluded his business and headed back earlier than expected.

Master Talbot arrived home just as the uninvited guest was leaving the house. William Glover's face had not changed at all and was instantly recognised by Master Talbot. Watching from the stable, Talbot saw the rider gallop across the field towards the road and stunned with shock he hurried into the house.

"What visitor hath ventured here?" he shouted as he entered.

"My dear do not shout so!" cried out the mistress, surprised and distressed by her husband's manner.

"What did he want?" Talbot asked, his voice shaking.

"Why he says he is thy distant cousin and that he was acquainted with thy brother who died on the road." Mistress Sarah began "He came to ask if it were true that the monk had died here after an accident. He mentioned Neath Abbey and an important task the monk had undertaken."

Master Talbot's face paled and he looked older than his years.

"What task was that?" he asked his wife.

"That he did not say, for I explained that 'twas all before I was even born." She stopped and held her husband's arm. "What is it husband that fills thee with such dread? I could tell him nothing since I know nothing. This is a matter we have never discussed; I know nought of thy brother or the Abbey."

Her words calmed Master Talbot and he sat down at the table. His hands covered his face as he remembered the King's men and their hunt for The David Cross.

"Thou art right my love" he said to reassure her "What couldst thou tell of this?"

Mistress Talbot hurried out of the room, glad for once to go into the kitchen and check that supper was being prepared. She put away her lavender bags and with them her thoughts of William Glover.

At the table Master Talbot was worried. What brought this man back to the farm after all these years? What trouble was ahead for the family now? Had they not paid enough with his brother's life? What of the cross? It had been out of his mind for many years. Only he and his first wife knew of it being hidden at the farm. Should he move it now? Did the man guess that he had the cross? What else would bring him back here after thirty years? Master Talbot nodded his head.

"'Tis the cross." he murmured, "'Tis the cross that he wants for sure."

Chapter Six

An Unexpected Journey

William Glover could not bring himself to return to the farmhouse for several weeks. When he did the seasons had changed and November winds were racing across the valley. The cold struck at his heart and strengthened his resolve.

Bethan was busy in the farmhouse kitchen. As the housekeeper was still unwell she was doing the job of two servants. Fresh plums from the orchard were bubbling on the fire in a stout, black cooking pot. The air was sweet and heavy with the scent of fruit and spices. Mistress Talbot had given Bethan a precious cinnamon stick to simmer with the plums and a delicious aroma rose from the pot.

John Talbot poked his head around the kitchen door and called out to Bethan:

"Bore da Mistress plums and custard!" he teased, pulling a silly face at the young girl. Bethan frowned and did not look up.

"Bore da young master" she replied.

"Yon meat needs turning" he called out nodding towards the lamb that was roasting on the spit.

Bethan glanced across the kitchen and gasped. She was holding the heavy black plum pot in both hands and struggling to carry it to the wooden table in the centre of the room. Wisps of long black curls escaped her linen cap and feathered her reddened face as she looked anxiously at the sizzling meat.

"Oh please help me Master John!" she implored "Pray turn the spit for me 'fore it burns."

"I am not thy spit boy" he answered, "I am no servant in this house!"

"Master, I beseech thee!" Bethan repeated, her face sweating with the fierce kitchen heat and the weight of the pot she carried.

"Come Tess!" called out John grinning spitefully, "Away to the fields, the kitchen is no place for us!"

The young boy and his dog hurried out of the farmhouse leaving Bethan to manage alone in the kitchen.

"Bethan!" Sarah Talbot's footsteps were scuttling across the stone floor towards the kitchen "Bethan that lamb is burning girl, I can smell it from here."

She entered the kitchen to find Bethan standing with her apron pulled up to hide her face.

The Mistress ran to the spit and turned it quickly:

"Mercy girl what's amiss?" she squealed, "Why the Master's good meat is burning and there thou stands with thy face hidden! Are we to go back to the mutton boiled in porridge that we had when first I came here?"

Master Talbot entered the kitchen too, alarmed by the commotion. He quickly realised that Bethan was upset.

"Hush wife" he whispered to his wife "look to the child for she is distressed."

Now Bethan was too afraid to lower her apron and face the Master and Mistress. She stood, shaking, as tears welled in her tired eyes and made damp smudges on her plum-stained apron.

"Oh I cannot do with these country servants Master Talbot!" snapped the Mistress angrily "I tell thee I have had my fill of the farm and am back to Tenby this instant!" She turned on her heels and stormed out of the kitchen.

Master Talbot looked from her to Bethan, who now peeped with horror over hands.

"Forgive me Master!" she sobbed "I am so sorry to burn the meat but I ......" she broke off and mopped at her tears with a small rag from her pocket "...I cannot do it all! 'Tis too much for me! 'Tis not fair!"

The poor child cried bitterly now and let herself drop slowly so that she was finally sitting on the kitchen floor amongst dried rushes and vegetable peelings. Master Talbot felt uncomfortable and unsure of what to do next. He moved slightly towards Bethan.

"Now Bethan, "he began "dry thine eyes and fear not. 'Tis hard on thee when the housekeeper is out of sorts."

"Aye sir" Bethan butted in "and she is always out of sorts for drinking too much cider and ale."

Bethan realised she had said far too much and was now in real trouble.

John and Tess chose to reappear at that moment. John's first reaction, when he entered the kitchen, was to laugh out loud. Tess decided to join in the fuss and barked loudly, jumping and behaving like a young pup.

"What foolish nonsense is this?" John shouted and laughed stupidly again. This enraged Bethan and she fled from the room and into the peace of the herb garden.

Master Talbot was angry now too, not with Bethan, but with his son and his wife.

He stamped out of the room with his face unusually stern and annoyed.

Master Talbot rarely lost his temper; this was not like him at all.

"Mistress Talbot!" he called "John! This is most unfortunate! Young Bethan is here trying to cook and clean, to fetch and carry for us all!"

His family stood silently, John hung his head and Mistress Talbot had lost her colour.

"Methinks 'tis time for thee to have respite Mistress." he turned to his wife and she stood in shocked silence listening to her husband's words. Many times she had complained to him about the farm and boasted about her grand life in Tenby, but he had never reacted in this way before.

"A visit with thy family is quite in order and in the meantime I shall arrange for a new housekeeper." He looked preoccupied and muttered something to himself.

"Husband" said Mistress Sarah looking close to tears herself "forgive me if I was unjust.........."

Master Talbot interrupted her "Nay Mistress do not be ill at ease, 'tis for the best."

"For me to leave?" asked the Mistress, her eyes now bigger and wider than he had ever seen them.

"For thee to take a rest! For thee to breathe the sea air again, 'tis in thy bones after all." He tried to smile and reassure her. "Maybe young John should accompany thee sweetheart, aye, that's the best idea!" He glanced at his son to discover his reaction to the unscheduled holiday.

John looked amazed at what was being said:

"Father, am I to go to Tenby without thee?" he asked.

"Thou shalt be a man and take care of thy sweet step-mother John. I durst not leave the farm at such a busy time."

Sarah Talbot turned quietly and tilted her pretty head to avoid her husband seeing how hurt she was at this seeming rejection. She cursed her foolhardy arrogance and her selfish ways. Now she must face the family in Tenby and explain her reasons for travelling in November without her husband.

While this conversation was taking place Bethan had crept back into the kitchen and was resuming her work, unsure of what the Master would do to punish her for the trouble she had caused.

John skulked out of the door and into the garden. As he passed the kitchen window he whispered:

"This is thy fault Bethan! Now my father and I shall be parted because of thee!"

There was real malice in his voice but Bethan was used to his unkind remarks. Usually she stood up to John Talbot but today she decided to keep her own council.

The meal was finally prepared and eaten, mostly in silence. Bethan kept well out of the way. The very last thing she wanted to do was to cause trouble for the family. Her own father had worked for many years on the farm and as soon as she was old enough Master Talbot had found her a place too. He was a good man and his new wife, for all her foolish ways, was a kind enough mistress.

At eventide the wind blew gently across the valley, carrying with it the scent of heather and the last woodland flowers. The sky softened from mauve to purple and finally shrouded the farmhouse in black night. All was silent, everyone deep in their own thoughts.

Master Talbot approached the bedroom where his wife was pretending to read by a burning taper. Her heart was heavy and her face puffy with crying.

"Methinks Bethan should also travel to Tenby with thee" he said gently.

"Bethan? Why, who would care for thee?" Sarah replied.

"I need no caring" he replied, "I shall find a cook from the village, perhaps Tom Fisher's sister will take a post here." He smiled at his wife: "Do not be so sad, truly this is for the best. On the morrow Bethan shall help thee to pack, send a message to thy father and then away to go! John shall keep thee company and Bethan shall care for thee – it will work out splendidly!"

Sarah Talbot put down her book and moved towards her husband. She pouted as prettily as she could and lifted her eyes to his in her practiced endearing way.

"Sir if I have offended thee........." she began and waited for him to respond. He did not. Sarah Talbot moved in closer, she had never before initiated physical love between them and was unsure and anxious. Her warm flesh cushioned his as she ran her fingers across his chest. Still her husband did not respond, his mind was preoccupied and he gazed ahead without seeing her. She turned away from him, her eyes now scorched again with tears.

"I should be pleased" she thought to herself "I should be relieved that I am spared the fumblings of an old husband!" But she was not relieved and the possibility of losing her power of attraction filled her with dread.

Bethan lay troubled in her bed. Would she never learn to keep her tongue still and her temper under control? Now there was real trouble, maybe she would lose her place at the farm with the Mistress away in Tenby. It would be a good excuse to get rid of an outspoken girl for good. Where would she find work in the valley? What was going to become of her? There was a fire in Bethan that would sometimes flare up and make her say things she immediately regretted. It was her Celtic way, her father had said, it was in her blood - but it had got her into trouble more than once and she wished it would stop tormenting her.

As for John Talbot - he was angry. It would have been perfect if his stepmother had gone back to Tenby and left him alone with his father for a while. The two Talbots together; out in the fields, hunting in the woods, playing cards by the fire in the evening and sipping ale from his father's tankard. Now the worst thing had happened! A journey to Tenby with this woman! Meeting new people who would notice his weak limping leg and make fun of him! This was going to be a nightmare!

The Master, of course, had his own thoughts. There was something that none of them knew or that he dare tell them.

He had returned to the farmhouse that morning to find the trivial problem in the kitchen and he had used that as an excuse to get his family out of the house. He had needed a reason because that very morning, as he had left the house to check that the labourers were preparing winter fodder, he had encountered William Glover.

William Glover, at his most threatening, bullying and determined. He had shaken the Master by his knowledge of his brother's death and The David Cross. He was convinced that the cross was still at the farmhouse or if not, that Master Talbot knew of its whereabouts. No amount of denials would put Glover off the track and the conversation ended with a threat:

"You have a son Master Talbot," sneered William Glover "a young son and a very pretty wife. I should hate to see thee lose them for the sake of a bit of gold and lot of sentiment! Think about it carefully. I shall return in a few days so make certain that there is good news for me, for I am deadly serious!"

Master Talbot had made up his mind. He would stay at the farm and face William Glover but his family would flee to Tenby – and with them would go the cross!

Chapter Seven

Towards The Severn Sea

Elizabeth Tudor returned from her Summer Progress and prepared herself for conflict. Her life had see-sawed uncontrollably taking her from the high status of royal princess and plunging her to the role of a King's bastard. She had been stripped of her title by her own father and imprisoned in the Tower by her half-sister Mary. Elizabeth lived in constant danger. She had grown up amidst treachery and intrigue and out of it all she emerged the glorious Queen. Now in her thirties, she was triumphant; the lion's cub, her father's daughter in looks and temperament, a true Prince with Welsh blood empowering her veins.

In August she had left Greenwich and with a following of servants, guardsmen, maids of honour and many others, moved her court to the countryside. Carts overloaded with items from the royal household rumbled out of London causing choking dust to rise from the deeply rutted roads. Outriders cleared the path ahead and the Queen's coach was flanked by men at arms and followed by privy councillors. Inside the gilded coach Elizabeth Tudor was carried to her people, that they might marvel at her magnificent clothing and strain to catch a glimpse of her jewelled hands and throat. To be seen, however, was not enough! Elizabeth must show them that their Queen could speak in many languages, addressing the people in Latin and Greek, that she could maintain a busy programme by tirelessly attending lectures, sermons and plays. The love that she had for her people must be shown to them that they might love her back.

When Elizabeth was in Oxford enjoying the play "Palamon and Arcite" the stage collapsed and three people were killed and some five injured. The Queen's reaction was to send her own surgeons to help the victims of this accident. She was rewarded by a crowd of people who cheered and ran alongside her coach for some two miles or more when she left Oxford for Kenilworth. This was Elizabeth at her most compassionate and most shrewd. She understood that her greatest allies were the people and the power they wielded maintained the balance of her throne.

Travelling was difficult and dangerous for a Queen in 1566, for an unaccompanied woman with two children it was perilous. It would take at least a day to cover a few miles over land and the roads were muddy, riddled with potholes and alive with thieves.

Travelling by water was the best option for anyone living near a river or the coast. Master Talbot accompanied his wife, John Talbot and their maidservant Bethan to the river Wye. From there they joined a boat that carried timber down to Chepstow.

"In Chepstow stay at the Great Oak Inn and await a message from Jonathan Fairbrother." instructed Master Talbot.

"Pray who is he?" asked his son.

"A man I have met around Llantarnum on my visits. He regularly takes boats in and out of Chepstow. I have sent word to him, but if all else fails ask for him at the inn." He could not meet his wife's frightened eyes as he kissed her goodbye.

"Dear God forgive me for putting them through this!" he whispered as the boat steered its way uncertainly down the River Wye.

"They be safe with me bless you!" shouted the Timber merchant to the forlorn figure waving on the riverbank. And mercifully they were!

The Bristol Channel, known as the Severn Sea at that time, was a busy waterway linking Britain with Europe and the New World, as well as being a trade route between towns and cities.

Great sailing ships, hewn from ancient oak forests, glided gracefully into Bristol harbour bringing spices, silk and dried fruits. Smaller vessels sailed the waters too, carrying coal, wool and merchandise from one side of England and Wales to another. To use the port of Bristol, however, dues and taxes had to be paid. Many English merchants, who wished to avoid paying these monies, used Chepstow as a distributing centre for cities and towns on the River Severn. The town itself, with its Castle built on the brink of the river, was a bustling, exciting place to be. All manner of vessels could come up the estuary as the tide rose to great heights; so high that the bridge over the Wye was built upon piles. This economical route for moving cargo rapidly grew in popularity and amongst the merchants became known as the 'Welsh Road'. Sea-going boats bound for far off lands also often called at Chepstow, Newport and Cardiff to recruit seamen but increasingly the trade was local; a regular coastal voyage to Tenby and Pembroke or a cross channel trip to North Devon and Somerset. Trade was flourishing and this was just the beginning of Elizabethan enterprise.

The November morning rippled the salt waves of the harbour and made the small boats dance on the water. Jonathan Fairbrother and his brother Mark regularly worked the boats that carried cargo between Tenby and Bristol. There was a daily trade along this coastal run and it was convenient when they were not working on the land around Llantarnum. Mark Fairbrother was busy negotiating a price to carry coal to North Devon when he spied three figures making their way towards a passenger ship headed for Swansea, Tenby and then round to Pembroke.

Fascinated by the travellers, Mark leaned against a pile of crates on the dockside and watched as they asked a swarthy seaman for directions. Sarah Talbot seemed flustered and the boy looked sulky. There was a dog with them:

"Why have they brought that nuisance dog!" smiled Mark "Well, well what a party they make!"

As he watched it was clear that someone else had taken charge of the situation. A young girl stepped from behind Mistress Talbot and was in conversation with one of the local seaman. She was wearing a black woollen cloak lined with crimson. Her dress was simple, a cast-off from her Mistress in a moment of generosity but suited her perfectly. The deep red bodice was fitted and trimmed with lace. The skirt was grey and skimmed the cobbled street as she picked her way through the rubbish scattered around. The girl's face was the colour of cream, although her cheeks were flushed pink as she listened intently to the seaman. Hair, dark and shining like jet, escaped her grey bonnet and bounced over her shoulders as she bent forward to listen amid the clatter of the sea town.

"Mercy me" mused Mark Fairbrother "I don't know which is the prettier, the young 'un or the fair-bosomed Mistress!"

Mistress Talbot waited nervously as Bethan conversed with the seaman. Suddenly Mark was jolted from his daydream in which Sarah Talbot was playing a leading role. The sailor was pointing at him and the three figures were moving quickly towards him, with Tess bounding noisily across the ancient cobbles.

John, still smarting from his father's insistence that he join the visit had begged that Tess the dog accompany them.

"I shall need her father," he had entreated "she is my only friend and she will guard us as we travel."

It was true that any stranger who came close to the boy was greeted with bared teeth and an alarming display of growling.

"Besides," John went on, appealing for sympathy "she helps me when my leg is tired, she lets me lean on her back.

John felt very young and unimportant as Bethan organised the business for his stepmother. He hated being small and weak. His brown hair and chestnut eyes were just like those of his father and he longed to be strong and wise like him.

This time Sarah Talbot took the lead. Stretching her hand towards Mark she smiled and entreated:

"Master Fairbrother, I am Sarah Talbot."

Mark stepped back, took her hand and held it for a moment.

"Good day to thee Mistress Talbot" he paused looking more intently at her delicate features and then asked, "How can I be of service to thee?"

"I believe my husband Master Talbot hath informed thee of our coming to Chepstow." She read the surprise and some amusement in his eyes but continued: "Methinks the message hath not reached thee…" she stumbled and fell silent.

Bethan came to her aid:

"We are lodged at The Great Oak Inn over yonder. We were expecting thee to call."

Mark Fairbrother listened with interest trying to place the name Talbot and make sense of it all. Experience had taught him that when in doubt shut your mouth and listen for clues.

"We are looking for a passage to Tenby sir." Bethan pressed on desperately hoping that all of this would come right. She could sense the panic rising in her Mistress.

"Ah!" interrupted Mark Fairbrother "Then that shall be arranged afore long. Now get thy sweet selves back to the inn and await my call."

When they were out of earshot he turned to face the seaman, who was relieving himself against the castle wall.

"Christ preserve me from idiots and fools!" exclaimed Mark Fairbrother. He slapped the seaman on the shoulder shoving him towards the wall.

"God's blood I've pissed on me boots!" The sailor protested.

"Aye and I shall piss on them also should thou bring such fools to me again!" Mark Fairbrother yelled, his fist threatening the seaman's chin.

"Poppycock!" answered the man "I have seen thee with the town trollops up against this wall! 'Tis not like thee to turn away two willing wenches, especially one so young and ripe for the harvest!" The seaman grinned exposing stumps of decayed enamel where teeth had once been proud.

The tension between them was disappearing. "Anyway thou art Jonathan Fairbrother so what's amiss? They were expecting thee. Tales of thy lovemaking hath brought the fair ladies in from the countryside now!" he laughed again at his own joke and together they started to walk towards the Great Oak Inn.

"I be *Mark* Fairbrother ye great bull's brain! Jonathan is my stepbrother and he remains at Llantarnum saying prayers and guarding the site of the Holy Well. Least ways I believe that's where he is till Monday next." They parted company and for the rest of the day Mark Fairbrother's head was so full of his own business that he thought nothing more of his meeting with the Talbots

.

Chapter Eight

Fire In The Night

Master Talbot was exhausted when he returned to his homestead. Worry and self-doubt hung heavy on him and he felt much older than his fifty-eight years. He was ready to face William Glover alone and never to divulge the whereabouts of The David Cross. The fact that it now hung on ribbon around his young wife's neck made it all the more important that no one should ever know of its keeper, until it was safely in Pembrokeshire.

The night of the sacking of Tintern Abbey and his brother's death seemed far away now. So many families had profited from the sale of the monastic lands and great houses throughout Wales had benefited from plundered lead, wood and stone. Master Talbot tried to weigh it all up in his aching head. Rich merchants and landowners left their homes in Wales and hurried to the English court to bow to King Henry V111. They were still there serving one Tudor monarch after another; receiving favours, advising, supporting and sharing power with the most influential people in the land.

"And why should they not?" considered Master Talbot "For the first Tudor King was a Welshman, born in Pembroke Castle and raised on Welsh soil."

That made him feel proud. Also despite the dissolution of the monasteries and the destruction of Holy shrines and wells in Henry's time, the great families of Wales still clung to the old religion and mass was said in many Welsh mansions when the doors were sealed against strangers. That made him even prouder! Now the new young Queen was on the throne.

"Dear God" said Master Talbot suddenly praying aloud "Dear God in heaven do not let her shed the blood that her sister spilled. The Saints have seen too much of it this twenty year or more."

The knock, which pounded on the farmhouse door, could only be the fist of William Glover. Master Talbot fell to his knees and finished his prayer:

"And forgive thy servant Lord if I have done wrong this day. 'Tis for thee and for thy Holy Church in Wales. Holy Virgin, Mary Mother.............."

He stopped abruptly as the farmhouse door was kicked and a voice shouted:

"Do not make me disturb thy family Master Talbot! Open the door for me and give me what I seek. That is all I ask of thee!"

Slowly the old man rose from his knees by the fireside and walked to the door. His hand hesitated on the great metal lock that had kept them all safe for many years.

"Believe me sir, I do not have the cross that thou seekest. My poor brother took the secret of its whereabouts to his grave." Master Talbot tried in vain to persuade William Glover to leave him in peace.

"Master Talbot" pleaded William Glover "I am not a violent man but if thou wilt not do as I bid then I shall break down yon door this night!"

His voice was calm and determined.

He had come too far and been distracted too often to lose sight of his goal this time. "I deserve this" he told himself "this is a treasure that should have been mine."

Master Talbot slid the bolt back and unlocked the door. The cold blast of air that accompanied William Glover as he strode into the room took Talbot's breath away and he staggered back. The warmth from the roaring log fire could not prevent the icy November winds from penetrating the room with a fearsome chill. Rain was pursuing the gusts up the valley; eager to hang on the freezing air and change the very nature of the night. Outside the skeletal leaves of summer danced a ghoulish spin and a stray cat slid out of the barn with a squealing rat in its mouth.

The two men faced each other.

"I saw thee" began Master Talbot confronting Glover's frozen stare "I saw thee on the road with thy tawdry men-at-arms. A hunting party after a poor monk on a broken-down cart."

"I had no quarrel with thy brother, Master Talbot." said William Glover "I have no desire to harm thee, but I will find that cross one way or another."

He moved across the room towards a large wooden chest placed innocently but dangerously near to the fireside. Inside the chest were the blankets and counterpanes so lovingly stitched by Master Talbot's first wife. Talbot called out to stop William Glover:

"There is no cross here I tell thee! There is nothing here for thee. My family are safely housed elsewhere, so get thee gone from my land!"

Seeing Master Talbot's anxious reaction when a move was made towards the chest, Glover assumed that he must be on the right track. He knelt down on one leg by the chest and lifted the lid. As he did so Master Talbot dealt him a sickening blow across the back of his head, which sent William Glover reeling towards the fire. His arm crashed down amongst the burning logs. Pain scorched the back of his hand. As he snatched it from the hungry flames the pile of logs tumbled forward in a shower of sparks and burning splinters of wood. The door, which was still gaping into the black night, was flung back against the farmhouse wall as a fatal blast of air fed the flames.

The fire seized it chance and licked hungrily around the oak chest. Sparks showered prettily over the assorted materials and landed in black pools which spread and engulfed the careful stitches in flame. Master Talbot cried out in despair and tried to pull the contents out of the chest in order to save some of the precious creations. He made it worse.

"Stop!" yelled Glover "Away with thee!" he staggered to his feet and stumbled to the kitchen in search of water. Smoke was now belching from the burning room and invading his lungs. He could hear Talbot coughing but could no longer see him as his eyes streamed and stung with the heat. He felt for a pitcher of water and splashed it on his face, hair and clothes. It gave a moments relief, just enough time for Glover to see that the farmhouse would be lost to the fire.

Frantically he listened for voices just in case Master Talbot had lied and there was someone else at the farm. He heard nothing but the crackling, roaring obscene burning sounds as the power of the fire destroyed the house. He groped his way along the wall and found the back door of the kitchen. The cold black night was like healing salve on his skin. Still barely able to see, he dragged himself to the front of the farmhouse and called out to Master Talbot:

"Master Talbot! Where art thou Talbot?" his voice was barely audible and his throat felt raw.

Master Talbot did not appear and no cries for help were heard. Across the sleeping fields the first calls of alarm rang out. Shadows were moving nearer to the farmhouse carrying torches, shouting and spilling pails of water. It was time for William Glover to be gone. He tried to walk but his legs would not carry him. On all fours he scurried away like an injured animal and found the shelter of a hedgerow. The prickly branches punished his back as he tried to hide himself and he felt blood trickle down his neck as vicious spikes stabbed into his head. He just needed a little time to rest, a few minutes to breathe the clean air and to realise that once again he had been thwarted.

The fire was eventually overcome and the exhausted fire fighters returned in small groups to their homes.

"Christ save us from fire" murmured one "'Tis the one thing I dread!"

"Aye that and the plague!" added his companion.

"Jesu save Talbot though" the first continued, "his face were burnt black as coal. There's a way to die!"

"Heaven be praised that the boy was saved and his pretty new mother!" exclaimed another of the party. William Glover held his breath and listened as they passed where he lay. In an instant his spirits rose:

"Thanks be to God I say!" remarked one "'Twas fate that they should leave for Chepstow this very day. Aye indeed, 'twas fate that the young Mistress and the childer be spared!"

William Glover let his singed eyelids shut. He knew his next move. All was not lost.

Chapter Nine

Friends At Court

Queen Elizabeth 1 returned from her August progress in 1566 knowing that her actions and decisions in the coming months would have great impact upon her life and her monarchy.

She had spent weeks in the company of her beloved Robert Dudley, Earl of Leicester, but on her return to London Elizabeth the Queen must take control of Elizabeth the woman.

The pressures on Elizabeth to marry were stronger than ever. Daily her ministers pushed her as far as they dare on the question of matrimony. Elizabeth Tudor, however, had no will to marry, she knew how her father King Henry V111 had treated his queens, including her own mother Anne Boleyn. She did not intend to lose her head or her heart easily to any man!

She laughed as these ideas ran through her head and mocked her own thoughts. It was too late for Elizabeth to hold on to her heart; Dudley had won that many years before. They had become friends when she was a child and he had shared her happiest days and her most secret terrors. As a man he had stunned her with his physical stature. At six feet tall he had made her look up into his swarthy handsome face, now he must kneel before her as his Queen. His lean muscular body thrilled her and his energy and wit matched hers. They shared interests, sported together and their spirits rose and fell in a union that perhaps should have culminated in one of the strongest marriages in the land.

"God's blood but I yearn for his company," thought Elizabeth sitting alone one night. A murmur of his name would bring him running to her presence but that now would be too tempting and too cruel. She visualised his animated, bearded face and the way a smile would play around his mouth as he whispered a joke to her or breathed an endearment into her waiting ear. He was everything the woman in her desired but that the wisdom of the Queen decided she must never have for her husband.

Winter rain splattered noisily on the leaded windowpane at Hampton Court as Elizabeth sat and considered these things. The rose gardens she cherished were bare and skeletal. Her counsellors tormented her with talk of marriage and the need to produce an heir. The most powerful landowners and courtiers around her jockeyed for position, wealth and status. Jealousy, self-interest and greed fuelled their debates and coloured their advice. Elizabeth was her father's daughter and no man's fool. She was fired with Welsh Tudor passion and strength but also empowered by shrewd English ancestry, which her mother had passed on to her. The peace of her realm and the strength of her monarchy rested in her ability to maintain a balance between peace and prosperity. A marriage to Robert Dudley would destabilise her court and perhaps divide the country. There had been enough of that!

Sir William Cecil, who was to be Elizabeth's chief advisor and dear friend for many years, begged leave to speak with her Majesty.

"Your Grace there is a minor matter of which I would speak" he began, his head bowed and his voice soft and unthreatening.

"At ten of the clock when thy Queen is in her cups!" joked Elizabeth.

The Queen neither ate nor drank in excess and so Cecil knew that she welcomed this light intrusion and could even jest with him.

He had absolute faith in her ability to rule, but in Robert Dudley Cecil recognised a real threat to his own position and that of the Queen and country. They had shared long hours in discussion on the matter and feelings had been strong enough for him to declare that he would resign if the Queen married Dudley. The seriousness and implications of that had left its mark on Elizabeth.

William Cecil looked at the regal face trimmed with tight auburn curls. Her make-up and dress were becoming more extravagant and theatrical every year. Her frame was slight, a matter of concern for her physicians, but she had an attraction, a fascinating unconventional beauty that pervaded those around her and left them in awe of her.

As he continued to speak she nodded to him to sit:

"My liege there is………"

"Damn thy good manners! Say it Cecil for I have pressing matters to attend!" Elizabeth snapped, establishing her control of the meeting lest he believe her to be weak with fatigue.

"There is one Christopher Schutz, lately come from Germany and bringing with him diverse knowledge and understanding of metals."

The Queen sighed. Her gaze went from Cecil to the door of her apartments, which she prayed would burst open at her sweetheart's bidding. It did not.

William Cecil continued:

"He is an engineer Your Grace, who believes he hath the receipt for mixing metals with calamine and somehow forming a metal which will bend and twist to make all manner of useful items."

"And this is of interest to the Queen?" she feigned disinterest since her active brain was always ready to hear of new ideas and discoveries.

Determined not to be discouraged, Cecil persevered:

"I myself and some other of Your Majesty's subjects have embarked upon an ambitious scheme but one in which you Grace might take interest."

They were settled. Elizabeth enjoyed these times with her trusted advisor when they might take some mulled wine together and he would lead her from the turmoil of government and prepare her skilfully for sleep.

The rain beat relentlessly on the royal residence as William Cecil talked on. Elizabeth seemed to listen to most of the story and smiled or questioned appropriately. He told the

Queen of an exciting new venture. A Wireworks which was to be built in Bristol but had now been relocated to Tintern near Chepstow. Christopher Schutz and his partner William Humfrey had joined together and with support from some of the Queen's advisors had searched the valleys of the Rivers Usk and Wye to find a suitable position. A fast-flowing river was needed to take the Waterwheels that were planned to drive the necessary tools.

"Methinks the people of Tintern will welcome the work this will bring them." The Queen commented "Is that so my lord?"

"Aye indeed Ma'am" replied Cecil "There has been little employment since the Abbey............."

Too late Cecil had overstepped the mark by even hinting that as a result of King Henry's actions the people had suffered. Despite the indignity Elizabeth had borne at the hands of her father, she revered and adored his memory.

Elizabeth rose to her feet, a clear signal that the interview was at an end.

From the adjoining rooms where the Queen's ladies-in-waiting were accommodated, cries of laughter were heard.

Elizabeth strode across the room and threw open the door:

"What serving-wenches are these in the royal household?" she shrieked like a fish-wife "Who dares to keep this royal Prince from her slumbers?"

Used to these outbursts of temper and bad humour the ladies cowered together, one was so afraid that she dropped the lute she had been playing. They fell to the ground curtseying so low that their faces barely skimmed the stone floor. They were silent. Elizabeth picked up the lute and furiously smashed it against the wall of the chamber; but her heart was not in this fight.

"Where is my Kat?" she cried out, her voice audibly breaking with emotion "Where is my dear Kat Ashley? She would not let these strumpets disturb their Queen!"

Turning her face so that her ladies should not see the tears that now stung the royal eyes, Elizabeth returned to her chamber. William Cecil tactfully closed the door behind her and slipped quietly away from the royal presence.

Kat Ashley, who had been at her side almost since her birth, was dead. The devoted governess, tutor and friend had passed away in the previous year and left a void in the Queen's life.

Elizabeth let herself fall until she was squatting like a child on the floor. Her layers of brocade, satin and silks ballooned absurdly around her slender form. The queen cried silently. She put her thumb in her mouth like a child and let the tears fall. The ceruse, applied to her skin to give the white mask of courtly beauty, streaked and merged with the egg white, which gave a final gloss to the skin. When the Queen lifted her hand to wipe away the tears she smudged the kohl that replaced her eyebrows and rubbed away the carefully drawn veins, which snaked across her temples.

She cried for Kat Ashley who had loved her and guided her all these years. She mourned her dear governess who had suffered prison with her and felt the blows of kingship at her side. She lamented her dear friend's passing and feared for her own future. The tears fell uncontrollably as Elizabeth Tudor remembered incidents over the past years.

There were tears of self-pity too as she recalled Kat's words of warning about Robert Dudley. On her knees Kat Ashley had begged Elizabeth to change the way she behaved with Dudley. Rumours about the pair had been spreading across the kingdom, tales of their blatant love-making, an illegitimate child born to the Queen and, most dangerous of all, accusing her and Dudley of murdering the Earl's first wife Amy Robsart, Lady Dudley.

"Is the Queen not allowed to love whosoever she wishes?" sobbed Elizabeth. It was a rhetorical device for the royal head was destined to rule the heart.

Straightening her back, despite the whalebone bodice that sought to break her delicate ribs, the Queen struggled to her feet. Her face was comically daubed with smeared cosmetics, but even this took nothing from her dignity.

Moving to her oak cabinet she opened a drawer and took from it a letter. The wax seal was long-since broken and the ribbon that held it lay loosely tied. She was advised in the correspondence that everyone was expecting her and Dudley to announce their betrothal during her stay at Kenilworth. She should be prepared, therefore for there to be outbreaks of trouble between the followers of Robert Dudley, who now showed their allegiance by wearing lavender blue livery, and those who were set against him. The leader of these men was the Duke of Norfolk whose men took to wearing yellow ribbons.

A sharp intake of breath broke the silence as the words reminded Elizabeth of how she depended on her spies to inform her of such events. She began to tear up the letter and as she did so she threw the pieces one at a time into a dish on the table. As each one fell she echoed William Cecil's words when he listed Dudley's shortcomings and the reasons she could never marry him:

"No riches, estimation or power;" she ripped into the paper and threw it at the dish, "forever in debt;" another piece fell, "a scandalous, vindictive man" her knuckles grew whiter and her jaw was tight but she continued: "accused of murdering his own wife by breaking her neck ………… or having it broken?"

The Queen stopped and let all the pieces tumble into the dish. She lifted a heavy brass candlestick and tipped it slowly until the wax ran and dripped on the edges of the dish. She lowered the flame into the dish of paper and let the fragments burn. When the letter was reduced to ash she carried it to her casement window. Was she sure that he was innocent of Amy Robsart's death? His accusers could not find him guilty. The scandal, however, would always be there for his enemies to use against him. She dare not risk her crown by being associated with that.

"If you can kill one wife my love," she whispered to herself "then mayhap you will kill another!"

She blew the dish and sent its contents out into the cold air. The rain had stopped and the wind carried the ash easily from the dish and into the starless night. The fragments fluttered and came to rest amid the rose bushes; now shiny black claws reaching up in the moonlight.

"Thank God that I have had friends!" she said and now she could smile as her thoughts went back to Kat.

Chapter Ten

News From Home

William Glover hired a horse and rode for Chepstow the very next day. He arrived in the town at the same time as the news of Master Talbot's death reached his wife and son. It was Jonathan Fairbrother who brought them the sad tidings:

"Mistress Talbot I am Jonathan Fairbrother and I think thou hast expected me these two days or more." He was welcomed into their lodging at the inn where a confused Sarah Talbot listened wide-eyed to his greeting.

"But sir" she said, "we have met with Master Fairbrother down by the dock and he is arranging our passage to Tenby."

Jonathan Fairbrother towered above her and spoke confidently:

"Nay madam, forgive me but I speak the truth." He pulled a note from his jerkin and held it out to her. "Look, this is the message sent to me by your dear dep…" he stopped himself abruptly.

Still Sarah's eyes were full of misunderstanding so she called out to her maidservant Bethan:

"Bethan prithee come into the chamber girl, John can finish that himself."

Following her orders Bethan appeared and stood beside her mistress who was now seated at the window. There was silence between them. John Fairbrother repeated his words to Bethan and then added:

"But alas ladies, I bring thee news enough to break thy hearts."

The shocking details were related several times before John was told and then Fairbrother respectfully took his leave.

"I cannot bear it!" wept Sarah Talbot "What shall I do with no husband to take care of me?" She paced the floor; she wrung her hands and all the time her thoughts were of herself.

"The farmhouse has gone!" she gasped to Bethan, as if the child had not heard it before. "It is in ruins and the land should go to young John there, he hath said as much at the betrothal!"

"Do not take on so Mistress, the fever will be upon thee if thou dost not rest." pleaded Bethan.

"Do not take on so!" screeched Sara Talbot "Do not take on so! My husband is dead girl! My husband and my home are burned to cinders! I am a widow woman at twenty-five years of age!"

Bethan went downstairs to the Landlord of the inn who recommended brandy for the shock:

"Take this aqua vitae to yon poor lass" said the Landlord's wife "and a sip of sack for the boy." She looked at the maidservant's face and realised that she too was suffering. "There, there, young 'un, seems to me that thou art the strongest of the three. 'Tis no good thee giving in to tears and suchlike. Take a good swig of the sack thyself and then get them both to bed. The morrow will be better than the night." She smiled and returned to the crowded inn where customers were begged to keep the peace:

"......for the young family upstairs have had grievous news this day. A farmer from the valley hath been burned to death, burned blacker than leather they say and...."

"Hold thy tongue mistress!" called out the Landlord to his wife "We shall learn more of this anon."

In the room above, John Talbot had curled his young body around Tess the dog. He could not believe that life could be so terrible; that everything he loved could be lost in a few hours. Perhaps it was a mistake; maybe it was not his father that had died at all. He let the sherry seep through his veins and dull his brain.

When he awoke it was morning. Tess was lying at his feet and around him were someone's arms. They held him securely and he felt comforted. Maybe Sarah Talbot would be a mother to him after all. As he looked up, however, he could see long black curls tumbling across the pillow. This was not his stepmother; it was Bethan their servant girl. John Talbot thought of the many times he had teased her, told lies about her and called her cruel names. Memories of the farmhouse crowded his brain and tore at his heart. He shut his eyes tightly and tried to block out the pictures in his mind. Bethan stirred slightly as she slept, her warm hand was resting on his shoulder. John stretched a little too and then tucked himself more firmly between her safe strong arms.

It did not take William Glover long to hear the story of the bereaved young woman and her son and to locate them at the inn. John was awoken by the street noises that spiralled up to his latticed window and tempted him out of bed. Bethan had risen earlier and was tending to her mistress. Below him in the street donkeys were pulling carts across the cobbles and towards the jetty. Folk without such luxuries were carrying sacks and baskets, dragging litters laden with hides or hauling barrows piled high with merchandise.

Right underneath John's room, the merchant's daily business was well underway. He could hear voices, some from other lands, some in his native Welsh but all speaking quickly and excitedly as the goods were bought and sold.

Leaning against an iron handrail at the end of the cobbled street, was a man. The only reason that John noticed him was because of his bright auburn hair and the fact that when John looked across, his eyes met those of the man. William Glover nodded and smiled at John Talbot. Tess, who had been at John's side all the time, barked and scratched at the window ledge.

William Glover made his way to the inn and spoke to the Landlord. A message came to Sarah Talbot saying that someone wished to convey his condolences. At first she refused to see anyone but after quickly considering that she was in desperate need of help, she agreed for the person to be brought upstairs.

"Bethan take John to the market and get sweetmeats for me, for my poor mouth is sour with all the weeping." She handed coins to the girl and prepared to meet her visitor.

William Glover bent his head as he came through the door. Sarah Talbot immediately recognised the shock of red-gold hair:

"Dear cousin" she managed to say, although her heart was already racing, "You have heard so soon of our tragic loss." She beckoned to a chair for him to sit beside her.

He did not speak. The wondrous fragrance of lavender and rose filled the room and wafted towards him as she arranged her skirts around her seat. She lifted her eyes to his and although her perfect face bore witness to her tears, her countenance now shone with expectation.

"I am so very sorry for your loss" he said sincerely "I should like to help thee and the boy of course."

Sarah Talbot could not conceal her emotion:

"Oh dear God thou art an angel come to save us from this catastrophe!" she blurted out. Tears of relief poured from her now as she stammered an account of what had happened. As she was finishing she remembered something that John Fairbrother had said:

"The folk who went to help douse the flames tell of a stranger seen making his way to the farm after dark." She paused and stared at William Glover whose anguish now was obvious, "Someone said there might have been foul play. They say a man had been seen by the woodlanders..........Oh sweet Jesus..." she raised herself from the chair and he stood also. "Oh cousin was it thee at the farmhouse?"

The longing between them was almost tangible. He did not reply but stepped towards her and touched her cheek lightly with his hand. Sarah Talbot fell into William Glover's arms as if she had found her resting place at last. Their passion was silent and more intense because of it. He took her savagely the first time without heeding the unlocked door or removing his clothing. Sprawled across the bed, he found her willing body and used it to slake his desire. When he had finished he arose slowly and walked to the door. He pulled the bolt across and prepared to take her again. Sarah Talbot leaned seductively on one elbow and watched William Glover as he undressed before her. His legs were muscular and tight, his shoulders angular and firm. He stood before her that she might see his naked body and know that at least that was honest and true in its desire for her. Sarah quickly unfastened her bodice and settled herself before him as brazenly as any whore might have done. His response was to fall on her again but this time their lovemaking was more controlled and she whimpered with pleasure as he aroused her.

It had taken William Glover less than a few seconds to find the treasure that he sought. From across the room he saw the cross around Sarah Talbot's neck. It was hanging by a length of thick purple ribbon and was so heavy that red weals were visible at the side of her neck. When, exhausted, she lay back on the bed and slept William Glover put on his breeches and pulled a knife from his pocket. The small blade sliced through the ribbon neatly. Sarah Talbot slumbered contentedly as William Glover dressed himself, drew the bolt on the door and was gone.

Bethan and John Talbot, finding the Mistress's door bolted against intrusion, assumed that Sarah was grieving and wished to be left alone. When they heard the door quietly open and footsteps going downstairs, they went to see what was happening. Mistress Talbot lay on the bed in a state of disarray and when the children saw her they were shocked.

"Thinkest thou that she is deranged?" John whispered to Bethan innocently.

"She is still sleeping, John, let us not tarry here but leave her rest." suggested Bethan.

They left the room on tiptoe but Tess the dog bounded in with less grace.

Sarah Talbot sat upright and her eyes darted around the room in panic. She pulled the counterpane across her and tried to gather her thoughts. The state of her clothing and the pounding of her bruised lips, proved beyond doubt that the furious lovemaking with William Glover had been no dream.

"Get thee from my bedchamber, thou filthy pig's bladder of a dog!" screeched Mistress Talbot. Her language and behaviour was so untypical that the room was cleared at once.

Sarah Talbot had one more shock to endure that day. The cross, which her husband had entreated her to wear on the journey to Tenby and not to remove until they were united again, had gone.

There were no more tears in Sarah Talbot. She was stunned by the way her fortunes had changed in a few days. When she saw William Glover she had truly believed that fate had brought him to her and that he would be her saviour. Now she believed him to be no more than a common thief, a seducer of women and probably her husband's murderer.

Sarah Talbot was growing up at last.

"Bethan!" she called aloud. The maidservant hurried into the room, twisting the edge of her apron nervously. "Bethan bid the landlord bring me water and some salve, in truth my body aches this morrow."

She was hardly out of the door before the mistress called out again:

"Bid her prepare three portions of the ordinary also, for we must keep up our strength if we are to travel."

John was listening and stopped Bethan as she was hurrying past:

"Wherefore shall we travel?" he asked.

His stepmother overheard him and replied:

"To Tenby John, there is nowhere else for us to go now."

Chapter Eleven

The Road To Wales

Elizabeth Tudor was short of money. Her extravagant lifestyle meant that she had to call Parliament for only the third time in her reign and ask for revenue. The Commons and the Lords had become agitated and frustrated by the Queen's refusal to name her successor or to agree a marriage settlement. There was a genuine concern that the country was in peril while these issues remained unresolved. There were also grave doubts about the Queen's health. She had become so frail recently; she suffered with her teeth, her stomach and acute frequent headaches. Her near fatal bout of Smallpox in 1562 had shaken the country and they marvelled that one so wondrously delicate could have such energy, such vigour and such a violent temper! Her ladies of the bedchamber were quizzed as to the regularity of her 'monthly courses' and physicians were called to examine the royal personage who they considered to be in poor health.

Parliament decided to use this opportunity to press the Queen on the question of marriage and the succession. It was to become an open conflict in which Elizabeth's authority as Head of State was challenged. They dared to suggest that monies would be withheld if the Queen refused to name a husband and a successor. Elizabeth felt that she had been put in an intolerable position and responded in a most arrogant, furious and defensive way. She agreed to marry and to take less money. Parliament felt that they had won this skirmish; in reality of course they had not.

Elizabeth was outraged, livid and alarmed. She withdrew to her chambers in a state of distress:

"Send for Sir William Cecil!" she ordered shaking with indignation.

He came cautiously, expecting a rebuke that may end in his removal from office or worse.

"My liege" he said bowing as low as his court attire would allow.

"Where is that place in Wales?" she asked, so angry that her teeth chattered.

"The place in Wales Your Grace?" he repeated unsteadily.

"Do you not hear your Queen Sir William?" she stormed "The wire place with the German bear and the fast river!"

"Tintern Your Majesty" Cecil replied, "The Wireworks has been sited at Tintern, a little north of Chepstow."

"Make hast Sir William and arrange for the Queen to visit the works." She ignored his amazement and continued, "A small band of guards will be needed and that is all. No retinue nor ceremony this is not a progress!"

"Your Grace" Cecil butted in as soon as she took breath "I beg you to reconsider; it is winter, you cannot risk the roads in this weather. Think of your health........."

Elizabeth rounded on her Chief Advisor, fearsome in her rage:

"Zounds if I hear thee mention our health again....!" She kicked at a small cushioned stool and sent it flying across the room. It cleared a path through the rushes and dried flowers that were strewn over the floor. The scent of sandalwood rose into the air.

"Madam I beg thee not to consider a visit to Wales of all places." Cecil pleaded in a tone bordering on despair.

"What meanest thou 'of all places' is it not the home of our forebears? Did not our grandfather Henry Tudor march to glory from those hills and vales?" she paused. "We should like to see this land. We should like to touch the soil of our royal ancestors." The Queen's voice trailed off and she fought to hide her swelling emotions.

William Cecil went to her side and put out his arm for her to take. She did so and allowed him to lead her to her favourite seat overlooking the lawns.

"How dare they push me thus far?" she questioned, her voice now drained of its former fury, "Who are they to debate the birth and death of princes? These are matters for God alone and not for mortal men."

"Your Majesty was magnificent." commented Cecil trying to soothe and reassure her.

"I ask thee as my trusted friend to keep faith with me." She grasped his hand as she spoke. He looked at the famously long slender fingers that were so often hidden from view by gloves of silk or the finest leather.

"I will Your Grace." He promised, falling to one knee and kissing her hand.

"Make good sense of it for me Cecil" she entreated, "that I might escape and be myself for a day or two. Let them think their Queen is close by and that all is well with her."

"I understand that these past months have been exceptionally taxing." Cecil offered trying again to comfort her once more.

Elizabeth sighed: "Indeed they have Sir William but Oh that is not it!" The Queen began to pace the room and again her anxiety increased.

"The small pox made me look death in the face and left my poor lady Mary Sidney scarred for life. My dear Kat Ashley hath died. I have spurned my dear heart Dudley and sent him into the arms of Lettice Knollys. The three who chase my throne are all married: Catherine Grey, Mary Grey and Mary Stuart. And the latter, Mary Queen of Scots has given birth....." she stopped and swallowed audibly, ".........given birth to a son while I remain a virgin queen."

Cecil was quick to intervene "Aye but the murder of Mary's musician Rizzio will cast doubt on her claim to ......"

"Hush!" the Queen whispered, "it will not comfort me to hear these things. I live each day with the threat of poison and treachery. It is too much for even this Queen to bear. Let me go to this land and find the peace of mind that I crave. Help me my lord to be free of it all for a few days, that I might find the strength to carry on. Use the doubles."

"It shall be done" said William Cecil. And so it was.

The use of doubles or look-alikes had been successful in the past; when Elizabeth's life was felt to be under direct threat or when she had wanted to evade the public eye for personal reasons. It was a deceit which was secretly employed but which effectively satisfied the need of the people to see their Queen and to know that she was in control in these uncertain times. The visual impact of Elizabeth's presence was such that it was possible to dress one of her trusted ladies in an auburn wig and the royal adornments. The heavy make-up was high Tudor fashion and relatively easy to emulate. A glimpse of the face in a coach or through a lattice window would satisfy most observers. It was an achievable deception but fraught with danger. Cecil knew he might need to put pressure on Robert Dudley to distance himself from court. If he and the Queen were not seen around the royal apartments for a short period of time, most would assume they had stolen time away together. He could manipulate Dudley at this time, to a certain degree, owing to the ongoing liaison between the latter and the Queen's own cousin Lettice Knollys.

The arrangements were put in place in a matter of hours. Four riders, sworn to secrecy, to accompany the Queen's coach, fresh horses to be ready along the route and a passage arranged to Chepstow. The Severn Sea crossing would take place north of Bristol, using the so-called Welsh Road to reduce the risk of the Queen being discovered. This was to be a private visit with no pageantry or entertainment, only a small band of people would know that the Queen had left her royal palaces for a few days.

Elizabeth felt the need to retreat to the home of her ancestors, where her grandfather Henry Tudor had been born. There she would rest and think, there was so very much for the queen to consider. In late 1566 the people had taken so much from their Queen that she had little left to give. She was the most royal of princes; she was a true daughter of Henry V111 in every way and worthy to be on the throne.

She was, however, human and in that lay her weakness and her
strength.

Chapter Twelve

Return To The Homeland

The heavy oak limbs of the ship rolled comfortably through the water that day. In the cabin Elizabeth listened to the creaking wood as it strained to take the pull of the sails. The slapping sound of the water against the sides was regular and soothing. Overhead clouds with torn-paper edges jockeyed for position around the winter sun. Seabirds circled with curiosity and trailed the wake hungrily.

With careful planning and a small retinue, sworn to secrecy, Elizabeth had made her escape to Wales and for a few days she intended to hide from the World and to reflect on her life as Queen.

Only the Captain of the sailing ship was aware of the identity of the special passenger who had taken over his cabin for the journey. He was an experienced sailor and had been paid in gold to keep his mouth shut and his eyes and ears open. He planned to do just that.

Unfortunately, he had no control over the events that happened about half an hour into the sea crossing. Port officials, aware that merchants were using Chepstow to avoid paying taxes at Bristol, pulled alongside the boat. They conversed with the Captain and after some objections demanded to inspect the cargo he was transporting. Elizabeth's men-at-arms remained out of sight until the very last moment. Insisting that they carry out their duties, the officials were about to board the vessel when two of the Queen's men stepped forward.

"Tread ye not a foot aboard this vessel" shouted one to the shocked onlookers. The weapons carried by the soldiers and their Tudor livery were evidence enough of their status. "This is a royal matter and not for the likes of thee!" he continued.

Suddenly the Queen stepped from behind them. Her regal stature removed any doubts as to her identity. Her hair was curled around her long narrow face. On her head a green velvet hat was placed at an angle amongst the piled auburn locks and feathers festooned from its ribbon trim. The high lace ruff at her throat was trimmed with silver and gleamed also at her cuffs and shoulders. She was wearing gloves of lavender calf leather, so soft they stretched with every gesture the Queen made.

"Be not afeared" she called to the seafarers "no man who goes about his business lawfully hath need to fear their Queen. Now get thee gone and speak not of this encounter to any man!" She returned to her cabin without further comment and resumed her reading, taking pleasure in the solitude.

The guards exchanged a look of surprise and one commented in whispered tones:

"That were a damned foolish thing of 'er to do, showing herself like that!"

"Aye," answered another "but she be the Queen an' she does what she likes."

The men from the Port rowed their boat faster than they had ever done; the oars slicing through the water like a knife through flesh. They raced back to the quayside at Chepstow where the Fairbrother men were waiting to do business with a merchant.

Mark Fairbrother noticed two of the men immediately and called out to them:

"How now brothers? Caught some big fish out there on the water?"

They could not resist his jibe:

"The biggest fish you're ever likely to see Mark Fairbrother and no mistake!" one retorted.

"In truth we have been mixing with royalty!" boasted the other. His companion signed to him to be quiet but the interest of the listeners had been aroused.

"We'll meet and take a measure with thee later!" promised Jonathan Fairbrother and then returned to his business.

The merchant led the brothers back to a side street where he had his home. They went in through the heavy door and stood in the first room on the ground floor of the three-storey house. The smells of the house enveloped them; hempen rope, herbs and spices, fine wines and burning logs from the fires. This area had at one time housed animals but for many years now had been the centre of trade for the merchant's business. It was the site of all the bartering, buying and selling and in the day was as busy as the bread and fish shops further into town.

The merchant's desk was strewn with bills and payment records for firkins of soap, hogsheads of wine and fardels of cloth. Here the money changed hands and the merchants met to discuss trade. It was the very heart of the merchant's wealth and positioned so that all vessels coming and going into Chepstow were clearly seen from the windows.

The floor was strewn with rushes and smelled of wormwood, which was thought to protect the occupants from the dreaded plague. The thick stone walls were decorated with frescos and in some rooms tapestries were also displayed. It was here that the three men discussed all manner of business.

Sarah Talbot had decided to discover the whereabouts of Jonathan Fairbrother and to ask him to arrange a passage for her to Tenby as soon as possible. She went down to the quay accompanied by Bethan and John and made enquiries for herself. She was directed to the merchant's house and so told the children to wait for her return and watch the boats and ships arriving.

John and Bethan, refreshed and longing to explore, needed time away from the inn and out in the air where they could forget their sadness. Queen Elizabeth had arrived safely but was waiting until cover of darkness before leaving the vessel and finding the accommodation that had been prepared for her. Her guards were closeted with her in the damp and now overcrowded Captain's quarters. The ship had a hold full of grain. Most sea-going vessels at this time were plagued by rats and this was no exception.

The children moved towards the ship, then sat and watched the comings and goings for a while.

"Pray what is that?" asked John pointing towards the entrance to the ship's hold.

"Is it the Captain's cabin?" replied Bethan looking around her.

"No, fool!" snapped John "The cabin is down those steps, I heard the Captain telling the sailors to keep away from his cabin on this trip."

They moved closer to the ship; curiosity now overcoming good sense. The vessel seemed to be deserted. They slipped on board. The door of the hold was not locked and John carefully lifted the great metal latch intending just to peer inside. As he did so Tess, who had been sniffing around the floor suddenly exploded into life, barking and snarling and running around frantically.

"Tess! Tess!" cried out Bethan "Be still!"

"Look out!" yelled John "She's after a rat!"

As the door opened a lean black rat had shot out of the hold and was darting around with Tess snapping at its tail. Bethan lifted her skirts and filled with panic she tried to run out of the way. John followed her and the rat, seeing a gap, raced towards the Captain's cabin. Tess bounded after it and as Bethan and John tried to catch and control the dog, they lunged down the steps towards the cabin door just as it was flung open.

One of the men at arms had lifted the door handle to see what the noise was about and was ready to alert the others. He had no time to do the latter for Tess and the two children tumbled through the door and onto the cabin floor.

What happened to the rat we shall never know, but it brought John and Bethan face to face with Queen Elizabeth 1.

At first the Queen was filled with terror and furious that her guards had been so lax as to allow this to happen: "God's blood!" she screamed at the guard "Is the door to be opened and all manner of fools allowed to attack us?"

In an instant the guards were ready with drawn swords and had encircled the Queen.

"Damn thine eyes man" she continued to bellow at the guard "now the whole ship knows we are here!"

The guard fell to his knees and the Queen swiped him across the face with a spiteful stinging blow. Then the Queen looked from him to the heap of bodies on the floor. Instantly her mood changed and she threw back her regal head in laughter.

"What in the name of King Harry have we here!" her bead bright eyes darted from one pile of clothes to another, identifying a young girl and a boy struggling together with a black and white dog.

Their shocked faces gazed up at her in silence; even the dog was calmed.

Three sharp knocks on the door broke the silence and the Captain was allowed into the cabin.

"My liege" he said falling to his knees "Forgive this grave mistake that so alarmed thy majesty. I know not how these children happened to get near to the cabin."

"Tess was chasing a rat sir." Bethan said in their defence "We did not mean to enter the cabin and we are most humbly sorry for what we have done."

"Are we discovered?" asked Elizabeth looking straight at the Captain.

"No your majesty," answered the Captain putting his hand on his heart "I swear thy secret is still safe."

"Good!" snapped the Queen "Now get thee gone and take these ragamuffins with thee!"

Bethan struggled to her feet but John's weak leg made it hard for him to arise from the polished wood floor. Tess, intelligent dog that she was, stood at his side as she had done many times and allowed the boy to pull himself up by holding on to her back.

Elizabeth spotted this and spoke out:

"Good grief thou art blessed with a clever dog young ruffian!" she said smiling.

John looked up into her face; at her golden hair fashioned high upon her forehead and twisted into plaits and curls right around the hairline. Although she was travelling incognito, her clothes were of the finest velvet and silk.

"Thank 'ee mistress" stammered John Talbot his eyes wide with disbelief as he began to take in the scene around him.

"And we can see thou too art a clever young wag!" she went over to the Captain's chair and sat down. A guard ran at once to arrange plump cushions at her back and place a small footstool under her slippered feet. She beckoned to the pair of them and they approached her timidly.

"Tell me truly if thou canst keep a secret."

Bethan and John nodded almost in unison, aware now that they were in very special company. Bethan went to look up but the Queen snapped at her:

"Do not look up into our eyes! Neither man nor woman dares look at us and be our equal! Thou have this day met with thy royal Queen, God's own chosen anointed one." the Queen paused and watched the wonder in their faces as she spoke. She loved children and did not want them to really fear her.

"Be not afraid we are a royal prince with compassion for our people" she went on.

As she spoke Bethan could not help wondering why she always referred to herself as 'we'. Only much later did she find out about the 'royal plural'.

"Tell no one of this meeting!" she ordered; her voice serious again. "Tell not a soul of our presence on this voyage, not even thy parents! I demand that thou givest this promise to thy Queen."

Still the two stood in silence, listening in awe. Then they

gave their promise.

"Art thou travelling to Bristol?" inquired the Queen.

"No your Majesty." Bethan said with a curtsey "Our destination is Tenby."

"Very well" replied the Queen nodding "then we shall not meet again. Now take a sweetmeat from this platter and get thee gone."

Bethan and John bowed their heads and holding Tess by her collar they emerged from the cabin. As they walked back across the deck they did not trust themselves to speak. Their mouths were flooded with the syrupy taste of sweetmeats and their noses full of the fragrance which had filled the cabin.

"Methinks it is sandalwood that smelled so sweet" mused Bethan at last.

"What?" said John "What are you talking about?"

"The Qu......" John burst in before she could say the word:

"Thou hast promised Bethan" he whispered, "it is a secret!"

Sarah Talbot, having arranged their passage to Tenby was returning to the quay.

As they approached Mistress Talbot, Bethan and John were afraid that she would scold them and question them as to their whereabouts. They did not want to tell her a lie but could not betray their promise.

They need not have worried for Mistress Talbot was too concerned with their voyage to her home. She longed now to see her family and to forget the incidents of the past few days.

In the merchant's house, the incident with the children and the dog had been witnessed by Mark Fairbrother. Looking from the casement window he had seen the events and watched with disinterested amusement at first. The alarm of the Captain and the presence of guards in the cabin, however, filled him with intrigue. He wondered what was going on and then thought back to the remarks of the port officials. Could it possibly be that someone of great importance was visiting Chepstow? He interrupted his cousin and the merchant to tell them what he had seen. They all three surveyed the dockside, but now dusk was falling and it was difficult to see clearly what was happening if anything.

"Let's get down to the ale house" suggested Jonathan Fairbrother "and see if we can find out from the sea-dogs. A few ales will loosen their tongues."

A heavy mist was rolling in from the sea; it hung on the old walls of the town and gave the castle an unearthly, sinister look. The custom's men, by this time swollen with pottage and ale, were ready to brag about what they had seen. Most of those listening were too drunk to pay any regard to the story, not that they would have believed a word of it.

The Fairbrother boys and the merchant were different; they did believe the story. They were survivors of the old faith. As they spoke together that night it was in the hushed tone of conspirators.

Part Three
Conspiracy

Chapter Thirteen

Your Majesty's Servant

William Glover had not left his apartment since the
meeting with Mistress Talbot. At last he held in his fist The
David Cross. Time and again he turned it over in his strong
palms, running his thumb along the edges and encircling the
rubies set in gold. He tried to remember why it had been so
important to him and moreover why men were prepared to
die for it. As the hours slipped away the realisation that this
was a hollow victory was dawning on Glover. His mind
debated the whole history of the cross. There must be great
stories and miracles known to the monks and the religious
men in Wales, which made them treasure this cross. In truth
it did not look so very special. He began to torture himself as
to the proof of the cross; who was to say that it belonged to
St. David? Didn't the religious men live simple lives? Would
the great Saint have wanted a cross of gold and rubies?
Would not a relic, a bit of bone or wood from the Saviour's
cross be more in keeping?

The memory of his time with Sarah Talbot refused to be
pushed away. The heavy-lidded eyes that expressed her desire,
the way in which her lips parted to welcome his kiss, the
surprising expertise with which she caressed his manhood;
these things burned his brain. He imagined her now; alone in
Chepstow save the son and servant of her dead husband. Her
home and future shattered, her trust and passion betrayed.

"Thou must leave thy conscience behind when thou
servest the King" an old soldier had once advised him. "Look
to thyself and no bastard else!"

It was a hard way to live. It had been Will Glover's way,
though he had fought many times with his better judgement.

Now what would he do with the cross? If he took it to be

valued or tried to sell it his theft might be discovered. Hanging by a gibbet from Chepstow walls was not a fate he wanted! His plans had been to travel back to his cousins in Pembroke and wait awhile before deciding on further action. Now there was a chance that Mistress Talbot would be in the area he dare not risk travelling there. He must go the other way, across the Severn Sea to Bristol and then on to London where he would lose himself in the city. The problem was that he could not forget his recent actions and his body yearned again for the touch of Sarah Talbot.

Queen Elizabeth had waited long enough and was eager to be on the road towards Tintern. A carriage awaited her and horses for her guards. They were stationed at the north wall of the castle, but a short walk from the dockside. Everything had been arranged for the Queen to be quickly taken across land to the home of Sir Thomas Herbert who would prepare safe lodging for the royal passenger overnight. It was a short journey but one that would take her out of the town and a mile or so nearer her destination.

Impatient for the cover of darkness, the Queen pulled a thick anonymous grey cloak around her, making sure that the hood covered her distinctive hair colouring. The guards walked briskly at her sides, to the front and to the rear. The royal party disembarked without bidding farewell to the Captain who expected to be generously rewarded once his passenger was safely back on English soil. Silently they mounted the ancient steps at the side of the castle, taking care that the Queen did not miss her footing or slip on the tide washed stone. Her small elegant feet were wrapped in kid leather and the mud and slime stained the soft material as she mounted the steps. Her many layered skirts brushed the remains of the day's toil from the stones and scattered it into the night. She completed the walk safely and without incident, her head as always held high and her mind alert. It was the first time for many years that a royal foot had touched the Tudor homeland.

No one could have expected that at that same moment in

time Mistress Talbot would send out her maidservant Bethan, accompanied by Tess, on an errand which would take her to the north wall. No one could have anticipated either, that it was at that very moment that William Glover decided to leave his lodgings and make his way past the north wall and down to the Great Oak Inn to seek out Sarah Talbot.

The guards recognised the outline of the Queen's carriage and for a second, as they approached it their royal mistress was exposed. The carriage door was flung open and three men (one guard later insisted it was at least six) burst out upon the party.

The first guard fell to the floor immediately. His throat had been sliced and blood was pumping from the gash below his chin. It formed a sticky black pool that gleamed and pulsated around his head. A second guard, also defeated by the surprise attack, lunged towards the coach but was floored and stabbed viciously. His legs kicked out in an obscene jerking dance as he lay on the floor. The speed of the attack and the noiseless savagery of it left the other guards terrorised. One fled for his life squealing and answered for his actions some six months later when he dangled from a hangman's noose in Chepstow Castle.

The skirmish was interrupted by the arrival of Bethan and Tess. It is unclear whether Tess recognised the lady who had admired her earlier that day or if she was just ready for a fight with anyone. Whatever the motive, the dog raced towards the scene barking fiercely and snapping at the heels of the attackers. This unsuspected intervention gave Elizabeth the time she needed. At the side of the carriage, horses had been tied ready for the guards. The Queen darted towards them, ducking to avoid the frantic blows of the men who were grappling together. One of the assailants was bleeding badly from the head and leaning towards the carriage in a dazed condition. Another was fighting with a guard whilst Tess bit relentlessly into his ankle causing blood to spill down over his shoe.

The third watched the Queen as she made her move and

pounced after her. An experienced and accomplished horsewoman, Elizabeth mounted the frightened horse and pulled on the reins. Yanking back her hood the attacker exposed her head which shone gold in the moonlight. Bethan recognised the Queen. Having been standing witness to the attack, she suddenly came to life. Looking around her she frantically searched the night for help. She saw nothing but could clearly hear footsteps running towards her. William Glover appeared at her side: "It's the Queen!" gasped Bethan pointing to a rider who was struggling with an animal near to panic.

William Glover was used to the narrow cobbled streets of such towns and cities; houses and shops crammed together with rooms piled one upon the other. The wattle and daub walls towered into the night until the top storeys of some buildings were so close that the occupants could shake hands across the street if they leaned out of their windows. They allowed little light to fall upon the confines of the north wall area.

He glanced incredulously at Bethan and then at the mounted horsewoman. The clouds agreed to part conveniently so that he could clearly see the features of Bethan and the brutal murderous expression on the face of the rider's attacker. The Queen's horse reared up on its hind legs as the man's knife ripped into its haunches. The Queen still held on to the reins, digging her heels into the horse's side and urging him to flight. William Glover brought his fist down between the man's shoulders with a crunch that brought him to his knees. As he dropped, Glover raised his leg and kicked out at the man's head sending him sideways and scraping into his face.

The horse tried to obey its rider but the wounds on its back were deep.

William Glover shouted to Bethan:

"Get thyself home girl!" and he kicked out again, this time at Tess who was snarling and biting around his feet now. The guards now all lay wounded or dead, one had fled the scene, and of the attackers only the one Glover had hit remained. He was lying helplessly on the floor twitching with pain. He looked up at Glover and spoke:

"If thou love the true church free us from this woman and her heretics!" breathed the man.

"What meanest thou?" answered Glover.

The Queen turned and yelled at Glover with the fury and frustration of a captive beast:

"I charge you sir to get me from this place if you value your life!"

Bethan called out again: "It is the Queen sir, come from England."

"Do you dare to stand and gape when the Queen's life is threatened?" screamed Elizabeth Tudor "Supporters of these traitors will be here anon!"

William Glover moved towards the horse who whinnied now in pain but was calmer through loss of blood. He put out his hand and the Queen of England took it as she dismounted. She moved towards the coach but Glover turned towards the remaining horses:

"We shall be faster on horseback if……." he began.

"Judas' bowels man just get the horses and take me from this place!" ordered Elizabeth.

Bethan was running back towards the Great Oak Inn with Tess at her heels, thinking she should raise the alarm. A small group of people were making their way towards the north wall. They were moving fast and obviously quite agitated but it seemed that they were unusually quiet and wanting to remain unnoticed. Bethan hung back at the side of a house. She pulled Tess in at her side and prayed that she would be silent as the men passed. At the front she recognised one of the men from the attack and as the others passed she saw that they were carrying weapons. When they were gone she hurried back to the Inn and told her story to the Innkeeper.

"Lord bless us what a place this is!" thought Bethan when she had retold her story to John and Sarah Talbot. She was exhausted by the events of the last few days and uncertain of what would happen to them next. In Chepstow, it seemed, anything   was   possible.

Chapter Fourteen

Escape Into The Night

William Glover and Elizabeth Tudor fled together into the blackness of the Welsh valley, their horses hammering the old road to Tintern. Memories of the night thirty years before, when he had travelled this road as a young man, worried his mind and troubled his conscience. They neither spoke nor exchanged glances. Every now and again Glover looked back to see if they were being followed but the night was turning foul and he could be sure of nothing.

After perhaps half an hour's relentless galloping, Glover reined in his horse and indicated to Elizabeth that they take a path through a wooded area. She followed him trustingly, knowing at this time she had no other choice.

"We must give the beasts some respite," said William Glover, looking up at his companion but being able to see little of her. The night was now cloud covered and the wind, which had spat rain in their faces, abated. With the calm came a steady rainfall, which soaked through Elizabeth's grey cloak and chilled her to the bone.

"Dear God forgive this headstrong woman," whispered the Queen. The foolhardy venture she had undertaken now filled her with dread and shame. They travelled on, William Glover searching the woodland for a blacksmith's forge he had visited once or twice. It was the only place of shelter he knew of in the area. It might be the safe haven they needed to save the life of the Queen.

The forest kept her secrets well. The horses were losing their footing as the wet seeped through the canopy of trees and loosened the mud on the path. Cruel branches leaned out and scratched at the travellers as they bent low between the trees. They would not let strangers pass easily into this sheltered arbour.

At last William Glover saw the outline of a building and smelled the smoke from the smithy's fire. He turned to the

Queen and stretched forward, taking the reins from her hands. She passed them to him meekly, her passion spent.

"Madam, I know not if thou art truly the Queen," the rain stung his face and he stopped, his breath now coming rapidly. Elizabeth remained silent. He began again nervously:

"I know not how to act other than as I would for any poor mortal whose life is in peril."

Still the rain beat down and the horses cropped the forest floor and shook their heads to show their discomfort. Elizabeth maintained her silence still further and her eyes, though Glover could not see them, were downcast.

"I shall go to the smithy for help but beyond that I cannot say." He dismounted and trudged towards the forge, leading the two horses. There was a dim light inside and Glover knocked on the door, calling out at the same time:

"Master Smith, fear not but open thy door in God's name to help a poor traveller."

There was no response but a shuffling inside and the sign of more candles being lit.

Again William Glover knocked and cried out but for a second time there was no reply.

Elizabeth stepped forward and joined the cry for help:

"Good sir, I beseech thee take pity on this poor woman and her brother, for we are lost in this woodland and sore in need of shelter!"

The door opened slowly and the blacksmith peered out, holding a taper out into the night. The rain snuffed it out almost immediately but not before he had glimpsed William Glover's striking features.

"Didst thou come here once asking about a young monk?" he asked.

"Aye sir I did" Glover replied, "and thou served me well with shoes for my steed and food for my belly!"

The smith stepped to one side as his wife pushed herself forward carrying a candle. The light fell on Elizabeth's dripping tresses but their hue remained obvious. The colouring of the companions convinced the smith that this was indeed someone he had served in the past and his sister; the likeness was remarkable.

The door opened fully and, to their relief, the travellers were allowed inside.

The blacksmith was a jovial man with a round face, roughened by the smoke and flames of his forge and reddened by a surfeit of good food and ale. He greeted the pair warmly and led them towards the fire, which dominated the home even when he was not working. It seemed that there was no better place to be on a bleak wet November night.

"Oh my sweet-faced child," gasped his wife looking at Elizabeth, "how glad we are to greet thee!"

She joined them at the fireside:

"My dear how pale thy lovely cheeks have become!" she said in dismay "Was it so cold outside, I confess I was dozing there..........."

Glover interrupted her gently:

"Mistress thy hospitality is overwhelming my sister. I have money enough if there is shelter and a little food we might buy from your good selves."

"Aye indeed wife" agreed the Smith taking in the quality of the visitors by the cut of Elizabeth's clothes "Find some ale and thy pease pudding or broth to warm their souls."

"She looks ill husband!" whispered the mistress as she broke two chunks of bread and put them on a wooden platter for her guests.

"She looks wealthy enough mistress," answered the blacksmith, "so get whatever thou canst to give them comfort for the night."

They ate the food thankfully and then Elizabeth approached the smith's wife.

She was stunned by the predicament she found herself in and exhausted. She dare not think what was happening outside; if news of the attack was spreading or if messages would get back to England. The danger of her situation was not lost on her, but she was no longer afraid.

"Madam" she began "Thy kindness is beyond our just desert. I beg thee, however, to seek out for me some change of dress, for I fear my present gown is so wet I shiver as I speak."

The smith's wife was startled by the strange accent with which she spoke. The smith's wife glanced down at her full belly and spreading hips; she shook her head saying:

"Bless thee sweetheart but my skirts be too slack for thee. I have my boy's hose that would warm thee through the night if thou art willing. He hath gone down to Chepstow for the fayre and ...."

Elizabeth was happy to wear anything that made her look less like a Queen. "Thou art too kind" she replied, "and thy goodness will be rewarded afore long."

Throughout that November night, William Glover and Elizabeth Tudor slept side by side on straw pallets just a safe enough distance from the smithy's fire. Neither slept soundly, the slightest stir of the horses, now safely stabled, and the snuffles and snores of their hosts kept their minds alert. They rested, however and by daybreak they were ready to make their way to Tintern.

"Why Tintern?" William Glover had asked.

"The Queen is expected there and we shall be safe." Elizabeth had replied haughtily.

Still wearing her borrowed clothes, they left the blacksmith and his wife. Elizabeth pressed a small pearl brooch into the hand of the wife as they bade farewell. Her host gasped with pleasure and surprise.

"This is for thy generosity and for the clothes" said Elizabeth with genuine emotion "Thou hast served us well in our time of need. God bless thee."

As the horses cantered through the woodland the smith's wife frowned at her husband and suggested:

"Something amiss with that, husband"

"What means thou? "answered the smith "nought amiss with a fine pearl brooch!"

"Aye but there's something amiss.......... she be no sister

to him, even though they both be golden haired. Think on her fine clothes and her little leather gloves."

"That's enough now" cautioned her husband "be thankful wife and don't addle thy brain with wild thoughts."

"Addle my brain indeed," muttered the wife "she don't fool me. There's something amiss with that................." and so it went on until the smith gave up and went out into the wood in search of kindling.

It was then that the second visitors arrived.

Chapter Fifteen

The Queen In Danger

By daybreak the rain had stopped but the morning was cold and damp. The sun gave a half-hearted promise of better things but no one was convinced. The Fairbrothers had left Chepstow at first light and followed the well-defined hoof marks in the mud. It had led them directly to the blacksmith and his wife.

"Dost thou think I am a stupid oaf like thy butter-belly husband there?" yelled Mark Fairbrother pressing the blacksmith's wife against the door of the forge. Her freckled face quivered with fear, threatening to crumple with sobs at any moment.

"I tell thee sir 'twas my cousin and his son that came to call last night, come a searching for my boy that was all!" her voice trembled with fear but her gut reaction was to lie. The Fairbrothers were known in these parts and young Mark was said to be a violent man and a bad lot. Angrily Mark Fairbrother flung her aside and turned to threaten her husband again. The poor man had been astounded when he returned, heavy-laden with wood, to find these men questioning his wife.

He glanced at Jonathan Fairbrother. Who he knew to be a religious and more even-tempered man:

"Pray Jonathan, reason with thy brother." he pleaded "This is our home not an inn to be bothered with travellers!"

"He's right" Jonathan called to his brother "Let us away, there is nothing here for us and we are losing time."

"They came this way brother, I'm sure of it!" Mark argued.

"Then let us take the path through the woods and into the forest" suggested his brother.

Reluctantly they left the blacksmith and his wife, but not before Mark had made sure the grip on her arm had bitten deep into the yielding flesh and left a bruise to bear witness to his call.

"A Queen without guards or a guide will be easy to find" Jonathan reassured Mark. "It is the Lord's work that hath brought her to our land. Now she will be made to pay for her father's wicked ways."

"She will be made to pay for more than that!" responded his brother viciously and he dug his heels cruelly into the flanks of his unfortunate horse.

Some miles ahead of them Elizabeth and Glover were moving steadily but the panic of the previous night had gone. Elizabeth believed that she was safe and as her fear subsided the joy of being free was intoxicating. They still spoke rarely which suited them both. William Glover was in a state of emotional confusion. On the way to meet with Mistress Talbot his life had been changed by a series of unbelievable events that had put him in the company of a Queen. Without choice he had effectively become a royal bodyguard and he had no notion of what the future might hold.

The blacksmith's wife had given them some cheese and a couple of apples for the journey. William Glover suggested that they rest and break their fast. Tied in a rough parcel behind Elizabeth's saddle were all she possessed in this foreign land. The clothes she had been wearing and her purse, which contained her jewellery, were lumped together in a damp pile and wrapped in sacking. She was dressed like a young boy and with her tall, slight figure she would certainly have not been recognised by anyone who was not out looking for her. It was actually Jonathan Fairbrother who realised that the youth-like figure was in fact Elizabeth Tudor and it was only because he saw William Glover first.

Elizabeth looked at the woodland around her. She was reminded of Hatfield where she had spent her childhood and where she still loved to stay. Her life had been cursed by intrigues and conspiracy; the fact that she had survived the past ten years was surprising.

"It is God's will that I survive this." she said aloud "He would not have brought me thus far, to set me down again."

She looked straight into William Glover's eyes and realised

with a shock that they were the colour of her own. The night had disclosed his features but not the extent of their similarity; she was intrigued.

"Who art thou William Glover and what manner of things brings thee to the side of thy Queen?"

They were sitting like two old friends on an outcrop of rocks.

He fixed her with a serious expression and replied:

"Art thou truly Elizabeth of England?"

"Aye" she answered and a troubled look changed her face and then disappeared. "I am my father's daughter; the lion's cub. But for just a brief spell I seek to snatch freedom from my duty."

"How doth a Queen snatch freedom?" William asked, "Is not the sovereign free to do as she please?"

At this Elizabeth's head fell back and she laughed aloud. The beauty of her striking features and the grace of her form stunned William. He was also stung with humiliation as he thought she mocked him and his pride was hurt. For the first time William Glover realised the range of emotions this woman could command and how, in a word or a glance, she had the power to make men cry with joy or weep in despair. It was then that the Fairbrothers attacked.

At the same moment William spied movement through the trees, Mark Fairbrother was suddenly upon him. His arm was tight around William's neck and choked him, threatening to snap his neck. Elizabeth jumped to her feet but Jonathan encircled her with a rope. She swung her head around and spat straight into his eyes, he staggered back and as he did so she slipped under the rope and kicked at his ankles with all her might.

He stumbled, knocking his brother Mark whose grip on William was loosened for a few seconds. William gulped the air like a dying fish. He levered himself up and jabbed his elbow into Mark's stomach. They rolled over the rocks together, Mark hanging on to William's neck still. William managed to pick up a large jagged stone and with it he cut into Mark's leg. Now in retreat, Mark drew a dagger from his belt and repositioned himself ready to attack again. Elizabeth mounted her horse and deliberately rode it towards Jonathan. Standing in front of the beast, he tried to grab at the reigns but she pulled back on the bit making the poor beast rear up in pain and fear. His front legs kicked out, sending Jonathan to the floor again.

With swift deliberation she rode the horse at him again and the hoofs struck out at his chest and trampled him as he lay helpless. Seeing the injuries of his brother, Mark ran to Jonathan's side and swung the dagger towards Elizabeth. It cut through her borrowed hose and left a gaping wound in the side of her thigh. From behind Mark, William Glover brought the jagged rock down on his head. Mark cried out and then slumped to the ground, blood oozing from between the stubby fingers that clutched his head.

Elizabeth and William escaped on horseback again, leaving a trail of royal blood that pumped steadily from the slashed leg. William Glover's heart was beating hard against his chest and his swollen windpipe felt as if it would burst. Elizabeth's leg had been painless but as the traumatised nerves recovered, a merciless throb of agony tore through her body. They rode on as far as they could but when she became faint with loss of blood and he saw her near to swooning in the saddle, William Glover left his own horse and joined the Queen on her mount. Supporting her body from behind, he galloped through the trees and deep into the forest. There was only one place where he could be sure of safety and that was with the forest dwellers he had discovered not so long ago. He thought of his last visit to them, it had been a different mission then and he had been a different man. He gambled that they might accept him and give him shelter.

The forest dwellers were busy at their daily toil as William Glover approached the settlement. They used every resource the forest could offer in order to make a living and feed their families. Charcoal burners, joiners, basket makers twisting hazel wood into containers and carriers of all kinds, potters, hedgers and so on. They worked from dawn to dusk and their world was a private place. William jumped down from his horse and led it quietly towards a group of dwellings that he recognised. The body on the horse was slumped and silent. He seemed to have arrived unnoticed, so he made his way towards the home of the woman he had encountered twice before. The place seemed to be deserted. He went right up to the entrance to her home which was now covered by a thick piece of cloth nailed to wooden supports and covered with some kind of rank grease to keep out the rain.

Softly he called out "God speed lady, art thou inside?"

He heard the shuffling of activity and then the woman appeared. She recognised Glover instantly and the memory of their last encounter on Blackberry Lane made her face light up with a welcoming grin. Before she could speak Glover put his finger to his lips to hush her and then spoke rapidly:

"Madam forgive me but I seek thy help." His voice was barely audible, the damage inflicted to his throat now seriously obvious. "My friend and I have been attacked and I fear he is mortally wounded. Give us shelter I pray thee lest our attackers finish us anon!"

The fervour in his eyes and the bloodstained body on the horse bore witness to his plea for help. She held back the drapes around the door and beckoned to William. He turned and slid the body from the horse, then carried it in his arms into the hovel.

William Glover's knowledge of women told him to pretend at this stage that his companion was a male. He let this lie persist when the woman asked:

"This is thy brother?" Glover just nodded "Thou art like two peas in a pod!" she continued.

The stench inside the hovel stuck in William Glover's throat and made him retch. When his eyes became accustomed to the inner gloom he realised a small child was sound asleep in the far corner, trussed up in cocoon of badly woven cloth.

"Hast thou money?" she asked, "I have scarce enough for

me and the boy, let alone two lodgers."

"Aye" answered Glover "Thy service will be paid for."

She turned away smiling. Slowly she then looked back and winked at Glover:

"Like the last time, eh master?"

The memory of their encounter burned between them both; she smouldered with longing and he fired with shame.

Chapter Sixteen

Days Of Freedom

The woman's name was Gwen and her skills as a nurse were only surpassed by her expertise in the art of lovemaking. Those first days in the forest were tense and emotional for Glover as Elizabeth passed in and out of consciousness. A poultice of herbs had been placed over her wounded thigh once the bleeding had been stopped. Gwen had pulled the ripped flesh together with her unwashed fingers as soon as they had Elizabeth inside the tent. Glover had watched helplessly and was appalled at the grimy hands dragging on the royal flesh.

He kept silent and watched as the lifeless body of the Queen lay at the mercy of a forest whore. The emergency treatment staunched the blood flow, however, and the mixture of herbs had an antibiotic effect on the wound of which all three were unaware. Bedstraw, from hedges at the edge of the forest, was added to the poultice to help the blood to clot and then scattered around the sickbed to keep away fleas. Strips of cloth soaked in a pungent smelling brew were then tightly bandaged around the leg. Apart from water, dribbled from a wooden spoon between the royal lips, no other medicinal action was taken for several days.

During that time Glover was seen as a 'paying guest' and the forest dwellers seemed to accept that. His horse had been tethered close to her home and soon brought neighbours asking to whom it belonged. Gwen was a consummate actress. Hearing them approach she pulled at her clothing and adopted her most lewd manner in the entrance to her abode.

"What rider have we here?" asked one voice leaning up against the doorway and peering in as far as he could.

"'Tis enough for thee to know I have a guest for now." Gwen replied.

"Well methinks he will need a good size pillicock to keep thee happy this seven night or more!" joked the neighbour

"And if thou needs a little help…" The man leaned forward and pulled Gwen towards him so that her bright eyes were almost level with his face. He bent his head and tried to kiss her.

"Fear not master carpenter," she replied, skilfully avoiding his stinking mouth, "he be a match for thee any day!"

The man withdrew, knowing full well that Gwen's tongue could be as sharp as her wit. She was able to fend off other visitors in a similar way and by the second day William Glover was free to be seen around the community. He was very careful but apart from a few inevitable remarks and jibes, he was accepted amongst them. The policy of letting nature take its course undisturbed meant that Elizabeth's true gender remained undiscovered for several days.

When her recovery was more probable and she became aware of her surroundings, William was at her side to explain their situation.

Elizabeth was the first to speak:

"This body is not as frail as we were told!" she said smiling, thinking of all the court physicians who had diagnosed her poor state of health and predicted her decline.

Glover sat at her side, as he had done for many hours.

"Indeed ma'am" he replied, "thou art truly the lion's cub!"

Gwen did not hide her disappointment when Glover confessed that his brother was in fact his sister. She laughed and joked in her usual crude way:

"Jesu, William, I had thought to have both brothers in my bed afore long!"

Elizabeth smiled thoughtfully and said, "Thou shall be free of men in thy bed anon, if our recovery is secure."

"Nay mistress" Gwen retorted, "I hope I shall ne'er be free of that!" Then she turned to William Glover and commented, "Thou hast a real lady for a sister William Glover. She doth talk like gentry folk not like 'ee!"

The weather changed in the following days and biting winds cut through the forest, stripping the trees of any remaining foliage and keeping the foresters busy. They had

Chapter Seventeen

A Cargo Of Oranges

In Chepstow Mistress Talbot, like Bethan, had spent another restless night. She spread herself across the smooth linen sheets and enjoyed the scent of the lavender bags beside her pillow. She was glad to see the morning sun although the air was crisp with the promise of winter months ahead. A fine layer of snow had fallen during the night but had now cleared. Life had seemed so very frightening since their arrival in Chepstow. Now she was sure things were going to change for the better.

"Let us go down to the harbour and watch the boats good Mistress." pleaded John as soon as they had dressed and eaten.

"Aye, my dear" said the innkeeper's wife "take the childer down to the shore, it will do them good to take the sea air. Mind that dog though young John, lest the sailors take him on board to catch rats for them!"

Bethan and John exchanged a sudden quick glance as they both pictured what happened the last time Tess chased a rat. He smiled at her and at last they shared something very special together.

Mistress Talbot prepared herself for a meeting with Mark Fairbrother. She felt excited and hopeful again. Just the previous day he had come to the inn and asked to speak with her. Sarah Talbot was well aware by now of the effect she had on men and so it was no surprise to her that when they spoke together he seemed nervous and ill at ease. She smiled now, musing on the way this good-looking young man wrung his hands as he spoke and sweated, his eyes afraid to look into hers. She lifted an oval mirror to her face and inspected her firm round cheeks and her lips, the colour and texture of ripe September plums. She was well satisfied that he should come to her begging to let him escort her and the children to Tenby.

"My dear brother Jonathan, who was to give thee help in this matter, have passed away after a fall from his horse two days since." explained Mark Fairbrother. "I have nought to make me tarry here and for the grief I suffer in my heart, I could not return to Llantarnum at present. It was my brother's last wish that his promise to thy husband be kept."

It was a lie of course. The dying wish of Jonathan Fairbrother was that his brother might flee Chepstow and evade capture and death at the hands of the Queen's men. Since the incident when the attack on the Queen had taken place, they had been in hiding. The Queen's horse had shattered Jonathan's ribs and both lungs were punctured. Mark had brought him back to Chepstow under cover, only to find soldiers everywhere and a price on the head of those who had dared to threaten the life of Elizabeth Tudor.

He had lasted barely a day, coughing blood and swooning with pain. No physician could be called and Mark had poured brandy down his brother's throat to ease him from this world and on to the retribution that was to come. There was no fear in Jonathan's heart for himself; he believed that he acted according to his beliefs and would go to heaven. Mark was left to fend for himself, all previous contacts and supporters having gone to ground.

"Seek out the Talbot woman" breathed Jonathan to his brother "then they will think thee merely part of a family. Get thee across the water and start a new life. The soldiers are searching for a man on his own not a husband and father."

It made sense and so Mark had sneaked out to the inn to take his chance with the fair Mistress Talbot. The vanity of the woman was exactly what he needed to make the plan work. They had planned to meet the following morning when arrangements for their passage to Tenby would be made known to her.

Tess sniffed her way down to the harbour, pulling John along by the leather lead attached to her collar. They had been warned about dodging the 'night slops', which were tipped out of the windows and into the street below, but not about the heaps of filth and rubbish underfoot. They kept close together with Mistress Talbot obviously feeling more confident and much more like her old self.

It was just as Bethan and John were hunting for seashells by the water's edge that Mistress Talbot heard a voice that made her heart jump and her bottom lip quiver with excitement. Mark Fairbrother was striking in new black doublet and hose. He still seemed nervous she thought but was smiling reassuringly as he showed her the bill of payment for passage on a sailing ship. He explained that they were lucky to get an easy passage at this time of the year and should hasten, as the ship would be leaving that very day. Suddenly the conversation stopped for they saw something very unusual taking place just in front of them. A small crowd had gathered on the quayside and were watching several containers being unloaded from a Portuguese ship.

"Lord have mercy what food is this?" gasped a fishwife stopping in her tracks and pointing at the cargo.

A sailor broke open one of the containers and pulled out an orange about the size of a small swede.

"'Tis fruit from Aveiro in North Portugal" he explained "I knowest not what they be called but the Captain says they be delicious!"

The Captain appeared and came forward to greet the growing crowd. His face was weather-beaten and his mouth flashed with gold as he spoke:

"Certainly they are delicious," he said drawing a sharp blade from his pocket. He took the orange from the sailor and with one swift stroke he cut it in half. Tess, who had been standing close, caught the spray of orange zest on her face. She whined and jumped out of the way fast, snorting and snuffling as it stung her sensitive nose. Everyone laughed and then gaped as the Captain bent his head back and squeezed the orange until juice ran down into his throat.

"Magnificent!" the Captain exclaimed "The most delicious fruit of all! Good for thee and good enough for a queen - for I am told Elizabeth of England rejoices in this fruit!"

In 1566 the very first consignment of oranges ever recorded in Wales, was landed at Tenby harbour. Part of that cargo had travelled on to Chepstow and now was being unloaded right there in front of John Talbot and Bethan.

Mark Fairbrother's face paled at the sound of the Queen's name and he looked quickly at the trusting face of Sarah Talbot.

"Then it is arranged Mistress," he said hurriedly "be ready to leave at four of the clock and we shall be at sea well before night fall."

A larger crowd was gathering and Mark was lost amongst the onlookers before Sarah could reply. She called out to Bethan and John who reluctantly left the excitement on the dockside. Had they remained they might have noticed a man from Tintern purchasing a crate of oranges and carrying them back up the stone steps to the castle. From there they were taken to Tintern where one day soon, he hoped, the Queen would present herself.

By mid-afternoon the Talbots were packed and bidding farewell to the innkeeper and his hospitable wife. At exactly four they met with Mark Fairbrother who ushered them aboard and by five they were at sea.

Chepstow Castle was silhouetted against the evening sky as the sailing ship leaned across the water and pulled towards the open sea. It was a romantic sight flanked by scarlet and amber slashes which scored the spreading darkness and stretched to the horizon. Sarah Talbot and Mark Fairbrother were sitting below deck sipping ale and talking. Sarah's head was bent closely towards Mark's and he seemed to be chatting in an intimate familiar way to her. They looked for all the world like lovers. He pressed his leg against hers and for the first time since William Glover had so abused her trust, she felt safe and desired.

John and Bethan had been told that they must stay on deck and try to keep Tess calm and quiet. By this time they were feeling hungry. They explored the ship until they came upon some barrels. Bethan pushed her hand inside one of the containers and found some dried figs. She pulled them out; they looked brown, dusty and uninviting.

"I'm not eating those!" snapped John.

"You have no choice master if you are hungry" Bethan replied and she popped one into her mouth greedily.

Tess was less fussy and gobbled down a handful from Bethan gratefully.

They tasted good, very sweet and moist.

"What about the oranges?" suggested John "Shall we try one of those?"

He crawled over on all fours to the large crate of oranges. There was a heavy wooden lid on the container and John struggled to lift it. Inside the smell of oranges was pungent and powerful. He reached in, plucked one large round orange from the top and carried it back to Bethan and Tess.

"The Captain used a knife to cut his orange," remembered John "Dost thou carry a knife Bethan?"

"No Master John, dost thou?" Bethan answered, very tired and unusually irritable by now.

"No matter" he said and bit into the fruit hungrily. Almost at once he spat it out again as the sharp orange zest sprayed into his face and bitter oil burned his tongue. He cried out, Tess shot up knocking into one of the barrels and Bethan fell heavily against the side of the ship.

"Who goes there?" a voice thundered from the prow of the ship and footsteps hurried towards them.

"'Tis rats that all!" another sailor grumbled, annoyed at having been woken from a deep sleep.

"'Tis big rats to make such a racket!" the first voice insisted "Give me a swig o' that rum afore I face this rogue!"

Tess saved the day again. She ran out from behind the barrels and began snarling and growling at the sailors.

"'Tis a dog is all!" declared the tired sailor, turning his back and walking away.

"'Tis a mighty fierce dog!" stammered the other as Tess bared her teeth and came towards him.

"Get back thou mongrel!" shouted the sailor bravely, but

Tess would not back off.

"She'll be hurt if the sailor strikes her" whispered John anxiously.

The Captain's voice now took control of the situation:

"What ails thee man?" he shouted "Can ye not sleep so the crew must all be disturbed in this manner?"

The sailor decided to retreat:

"Forgive me Capt'n" he replied, "I was mistaken, 'tis just the rats and a yapping dog!"

"Well prithee keep watch for we have cargo and passengers aboard. There should be no one in this part of the ship till we reach Bristol!" said the Captain.

Bethan and John, afraid that again they would find themselves in a forbidden part of a ship, hurried down to the lower deck to find Mistress Talbot. She was laughing with a flushed girlish grin that made her look foolish in Bethan's eyes.

John, still tortured by the death of his father just a short while before, was angry.

"Madam!" he said rudely "Dost thou think to make merry an' my father not yet cold?" The impudence of the boy and the fervour with which he spoke shocked Sara Talbot, but the actions of Mark Fairbrother astounded her. Stretching forward he hit the boy full in the face and sent him reeling across the deck. Silence followed, as those around looked on aghast. It was commonplace to chastise children but this man had served the boy an overwhelming blow.

Sarah cried out but remained seated, seeming afraid to intervene. Bethan ran to John and supported him in her arms. Tears and blood mingled as they traced across his young face. Still the boy was defiant:

"Pray tell me sir, why this ship is heading for Bristol when we are bound for Tenby!"

"What?" stammered Sarah "What meanest thou John?"

Mark Fairbrother rose to his feet and made towards the boy to beat him again. Tess dropped her shoulders low and growled menacingly at Mark.

"Cease this folly I beg thee!" cried Sarah "Come Mark sit thee down and let me see the boy."

Mark, his senses now dulled by cheap ale obeyed, while Sarah fussed around John and helped Bethan to comfort him. There was nowhere to hide on this ship; they had to stay together until they reached Tenby.

"Not long now," thought Sarah Talbot "afore I see my dear father and mother again. I swear to God that I shall ne'er leave their loving household again once we are safely home!" She dabbed away tears with her kerchief. The perfume of lavender and rose was still there, so she held it to her nose and inhaled the loving fragrance, which she cherished.

Bethan reviewed the events of the day as she sat, still holding John in her arms. She was very suspicious and afraid. The events of the last weeks had changed her, making her insecure and anxious. She had witnessed violence and become aware of deceit; the like of which she would have never seen had she remained safely on the Talbot Farm.

She was, however, learning how to hide her feelings to protect herself and others.

Mark Fairbrother shouted to her:

"Hey, miss Bethan, thou mistress busybody!" his words were becoming slurred, "Give this to the boy to make amends."

He pulled an orange from his pocket and handed it to the young girl. She took it without meeting his eyes or responding. Sarah looked bemused.

John went to speak but Bethan cupped her hand over his bruised swollen mouth and whispered: "Hush, say nothing John 'till we are safely gone from this ship."

Mark was watching them.

"Go on!" he bawled "eat the damn fruit!"

Bethan and John discovered that by breaking open the orange, sweet, juicy flesh was revealed. Her slender fingers prised the flesh apart and she handed some to here Mistress.

Sarah put it to her lips. It tasted delicious. Her pink tongue skimmed across her mouth catching the drops that hung from her bottom lip and threatened to dribble to her chin.

"I love it" she declared, biting into the fresh tangy fruit. "'Tis no wonder the Queen doth love the fruit!"

The innocent words stung Mark and he pulled Sarah towards him. Pressing his mouth over hers he thrust his tongue between her lips in a motion that was akin to violence. Her eyes shot open wide as his hand went to her breast and squeezed it, pinching the nipple in a cruel sadistic way. She leaned back and muffled sounds of alarm escaped from her throat. As he withdrew his mouth Mark's teeth were visible. Spitefully he bit into Sarah's lips and tears again filled her eyes.

"Just tasting the juice." he snarled as he turned away from her.

Sarah Talbot wondered how she could ever have been attracted to this man. With disgust she realised that again she had been naïve enough to trust a handsome face. Her self-loathing was returning but her ordeal was not ended.

Sarah watched Mark's face as he turned away from her and saw lust in his eyes. The ale and probably tiredness too, had revealed the man's true nature. He was capable of cruelty and probably worse. He looked back at her for a second and mouthed:

"Thou thinkest I desire thee but I do not!" his breath was sour and hot "Thou thinkest I would bed thee, but I would not!"

He turned from her, lust still burning in his eyes and with horror she realised where his gaze had fallen.

Bethan's eyes met his with contempt.

"She is only thirteen years old!" gasped Sarah.

"My mother was but thirteen when she was wed." Mark replied softly.

"Thou shalt not touch her!" threatened Sarah, her body now shaking with emotion.

"Oh shall I not Mistress Talbot?" Mark replied unsteadily, getting to his feet

"Methinks I shall."

He got up and staggered through the groups of passengers huddled around the lower deck. Some were sleeping, some playing cards, some drinking and sharing tales of other nights at sea.

Bethan spoke first:

"Mistress do not take on so" she tried to speak in a reassuring way "We shall all be safe in Tenby."

"Aye Bethan" answered Sarah "'Tis true enough, we shall all be safe at home in Tenby."

Just then a bell rang on deck and there was a burst of action and conversation. All the passengers looked up expectantly as a sailor appeared on the ladder leading to the lower deck.

"All passengers be ready to leave the ship!" came the order.

"Are we arrived in Bristol already?" one sleepy voice enquired.

"'Tis in our sights." was the reply "Thou shalt be safely landed at Bristol by daybreak!"

"In Bristol" exclaimed Sarah "We are bound for Tenby!"

"Then thou hast journeyed East instead of West young lady!" came the answer.

The   extent   of   the   deceit   was   uncovered.

Chapter Eighteen

Escape To England

Sarah Talbot realised with alarm that she had been used yet again. The real reason for Mark Fairbrother's deceit was unknown to her; she therefore could only surmise that his taste for young girls was the driving force in bringing them to Bristol. She was devastated by another blow to her self-esteem and appalled at the possibility of Bethan being in such danger.

The prospect of being alone in a strange country with the responsibility of her stepson and maidservant filled her with panic. Passengers on the lower deck began shuffling around, gathering their belongings together and moving towards the stairs ready for embarkation. Sarah had to express her fears to Bethan:

"Hark Bethan" she began "listen well to me I prithee, for I fear we are all in danger." Sarah's shocked face was sweating and she wrung her soft pink hands with anxiety. She looked from Bethan's dark eyes to the bruised face of John Talbot.

"Why did we come to Bristol Mistress?" begged Bethan.

"Oh child we have been tricked," tears glistened in the trusting soft eyes as Sarah imparted her worst fears: "I have been fooled by Mark Fairbrother and I know not the reason for it other than........." She stopped, unable to explain to Bethan the picture she had in her mind of this brutal man assaulting the young girl. "We must leave the ship without him." Sarah continued when she had her emotions under control again. "Escape is all I can think of for now."

John, still stunned by the blow Fairbrother had dealt him, clung on to Tess with one hand and Mistress Talbot with the other. Unsteadily, his weak leg almost useless after the reeling blow had flung him to the floor, he clutched at his stepmother's skirts. Bethan held the dog's collar and carried bags in her other hand.

"Keep thy head low and let the crowd lead us," suggested

Bethan sensibly "I have spied Master Fairbrother dozing in the corner. We might make our escape while he rests."

Those who had witnessed Fairbrother's attack on John stepped aside and let them through to the steps leading up to the main deck. Others were eager to let Tess pass in case she carried plague or other such terrors. They successfully made their way to the fresh morning air and the shock of it roused John and renewed his strength.

The sailing ship moved gracefully towards the busy port, even in such frightening circumstances the splendour of the sight captivated the Talbot family. A strong wind had brought the vessel to port swiftly and the quay was alive with travellers and traders ready to view the ship's cargo. As they drew alongside the stone landing stage, other vessels dipped in the sheltered waters and gave up their goods to the eager merchants. The crowd, the colours and the atmosphere of this prosperous place was unlike anything Sarah Talbot and her charges had witnessed before. Jostled by their excited fellow passengers they cautiously left the ship and went towards the narrow streets of Bristol. They had abandoned luggage they could not carry and were making good progress when Bethan suddenly was yanked backwards. Sarah and John turned, just as Tess's bark sounded the alarm and announced the return of Mark Fairbrother.

"Slippery as an eel this young 'un" Fairbrother said between clenched teeth. He had hold of Bethan's arm now and she was struggling, her black hair untamed across her shoulders and her eyes wild with fear.

"Let us be Mark Fairbrother!" Sarah called out "We have been misused enough!" Her voice was choked with emotion and tears began to stream down her face.

"Now, now Mistress Talbot" he went on, his probing fingers biting deep into Bethan's flesh. "Thou art alone and at the mercy of this city. Methinks there is little money left in that pretty purse thou art holding to thy bosom."

He relaxed his grip slightly and Bethan stopped struggling. He was staring into Sarah's eyes and his look was cold and merciless.

"Are we not a family now Sarah, eh?" he moved closer towards her. He stank of stale sweat and ale. He slid his arm around Bethan's shoulders and pulled her to him, still holding Sarah with his eyes.

"Dost thou know what happens to young women alone in a city Mistress Talbot?" he grinned and let his hand drop down towards Bethan's neck. Then he turned his eyes towards the young girl and stroked her cheek with his finger.

"Don't be a ninny now," his hand cupped Bethan's face as he spoke "no need for thee to fear, as long as we understand each other." He turned his face towards Sarah with a smile that assumed victory and control.

Bethan looked at her mistress's distraught face and guessed the nature of Fairbrother's intent, although the details thankfully were beyond her experience. Tossing her hair back from her face she twisted her neck round and bit into the hand that was caressing her skin. He yelped in pain like a dog and stepped back pulling his hand away. Tess started to yap and snap around his ankles while John, seeing his opportunity for revenge, kicked out with his strong leg and struck out painfully into Fairbrother's shin. The man, unbalanced by the trio of assault, staggered and lost his footing close to a low wall that skirted the quay. The final blow was Sarah's. Still smarting from the depth of his trickery and revolted by his suggestive remarks, she lunged towards him and with all her strength pushed him over the wall.

It was but a short fall and his head hit the cobbled quayside below within seconds. The thud of skull on stone and the sight of a twisted broken body attracted sightseers at once. Fascinated by the gory splash of crimson on the mossy cobbles they stared down at Mark Fairbrother's lifeless body. Mercifully, the three pale faces that were peering over the wall remained unnoticed. Sarah Talbot was open-mouthed and aghast; Bethan was appalled but ready to flee.

"Quick Mistress, pick up the boy if thou canst and run!" she grabbed the bags and they fled away from the wall and into the market place.

When they could run no longer they leaned against an ancient wall and waited, chests heaving and gasping for air, watching for those who may be chasing after them.

No one came. After a few minutes they began to relax and breathe steadily. John was recovered now and holding Tess in a challenging manner, ashamed that he had needed to be carried and ready to defend Sarah and Bethan against anyone who might be in pursuit of them.

At the far end of the market an old man and his wife were unloading cheeses from a cart. Bethan looked to her mistress and asked:

"Do we have money for food?" Sarah nodded and handed her purse to Bethan.

She returned with cheese for them all and a lump of black bread, which she broke and shared. They squatted like beggars at the side of the street with worried faces and furtive eyes. Sarah Talbot watched the old couple and savoured the creamy tang of fresh goats' cheese. She waited until all the cheese was unloaded from the cart and taken to various stallholders. Some market traders paid in coins, others gave meat and goods in return for the dairy produce. It seemed that the old man and his wife were not going to stay at market, but having delivered and sold their cheeses, were preparing to leave the city. John and Bethan watched as Sarah walked over to the couple and spoke with them. After a brief conversation she turned and beckoned to the children to join her. They did so and were relieved when Sarah, her tears now gone, said:

"Jump up on the cart! These kind people will carry us out of the city and into the countryside. Come quickly it is our only chance of escape, we are bound to be found and charged with murder if we stay!"

And so it was that Sarah Talbot, with John, Bethan and Tess found themselves in England. They were totally alone, apart from two strangers with whom they travelled the road, and with very little money left their prospects were bleak.

Convinced that there was no going back, lest they be imprisoned, Sarah decided that they must go forward, for the time being at least. The events of the last few weeks had changed Sarah Talbot stripping away her trust, her security and her faith. She resolved that she would never again let her defences fall. From now on she would fend for herself; assuming they escaped the charge of murder and public hanging. It was to be a long hard road for them all, but as they made their way westwards, their hopes were high.

Chapter Nineteen

Oranges For The Queen

William Glover took his leave of Tintern and turned his horse to the familiar road that led back to the forest. Across the valley the morning sun streaked, pushing arrows of golden light through the autumn daybreak. The winding mud track roused itself in response to the warm glow and disturbed the icy mist that clung to its shoulders like a parasite. The narrow bridge that took the rider from the main road and into the ancient forest remained defiant although the clear black night had frozen its joints and bit into its curved spine. A tunnel of branches that had once made a heavy green canopy across the road now leaned with stripped fingers towards each other. The searching morning light fell on the burnished leaves and gilded them for a last time before they must tumble to the ground. Where the branches failed to meet, frost seeped in and black ice had imbedded itself secretly during the night. It waited like a predator for an unsuspecting victim; it waited like a traitor for an inexperienced rider or an old cart with worn wheels.

William Glover tried to imagine the young monk, who many years before had driven across this treacherous route, fleeing to the safety of the Talbot smallholding. He thought of The David Cross which he had carried secretly and which had cost him his life. For the past week that cross had hung around the neck of William Glover and amidst all the turmoil of the last few days it had been out of his thoughts. His hand reached up and felt beneath his leather jerkin to check that it was still safe. He felt its straight metal edges which were warm against his skin. The feel of the precious stones reassured and disturbed him as he remembered how he had won this prize. A soldier could justify his actions easily in the heat of battle or in the service of his master. Which master did William honour when he took The David Cross?

The mission to Tintern had been successful. Following the

Queen's instructions, he had made his way to the tinworks and contacted the named gentlemen on her letters. Having read the documents there was a flurry of activity, riders sent away on fast horses and by water to carry news and information to England; to the very highest in the land. The royal instructions were that her whereabouts remain secret until she was well enough to travel. In due course Glover would send word to Chepstow and the Queen would leave the forest under armed guard. In the meantime, the less people who knew of her presence in Wales the better.

When William Glover was preparing to leave, his horse was piled with food, a leather flask of wine and clean riding clothes for her majesty. An emerald kirtle woven from Welsh wool and lined with deep purple, a strait-laced bodice and velvet jerkin fashioned in a deeper green and trimmed with fur. A smock of finest cream linen to smooth the royal skin, a petticoat and underkirtle to protect the noble limbs from the winter chill. A woollen bonnet to warm the regal head but discreetly hidden by a fashionable broad brimmed hat trimmed with small but vibrant feathers. Gloves of purple leather hurriedly brought from Bristol and a thick tweed shawl to drape around the noble shoulders. Everything had been rapidly found and prepared for the Queen's comfort on her journey back to England. Among the gifts of food was a small sack of oranges, fresh from Chepstow.

"Take these strange fruits to the Queen," ordered one very anxious official "for I have been told that she is enamoured of the juice. Let them be squeezed and the juice trickled down the royal throat. If she wishes, let a little good Welsh honey be mixed with the liquid to soothe her and speed her recovery."

When Glover arrived back at Gwen's forest home he was alarmed by the pallor of the Queen. Gwen was sitting outside the dwelling with her child when he arrived. She was washing some clothing in a leaky wooden pail. A small fire was burning at her side and over it she had placed some iron rods to make a simple stove. A kettle of water spat and simmered above the fire. Gwen poured warm water into the pail when the water's icy bite was too much for her fingers to bear. She was chatting in Welsh to the child as she worked and was surprised to see William Glover arrive.

"Welcome back my gold-haired rider!" she teased, unable to hide her pleasure at seeing him again.

"Good-day Gwen." Glover replied and brushing past her to get inside asked: "Is all well with thee?"

"Is all well with thy sister thou dost mean!" Gwen responded sarcastically.

It was then that he espied Elizabeth lying like a corpse in the half-light of the home.

"Jesu she looks ill!" he gasped.

"She is always as white faced as a lady of the court!" snapped Gwen.

"Aye she is pale," he conceded "but she is hardly breathing woman!"

Gwen came to stand beside him and touched his shoulder in an intimate act of reassurance.

"Last night I gave her a special brew to help her sleep. She will heal when she doth sleep."

As she was speaking William Glover noticed movement outside the door and suddenly remembered the child.

"Look to the child Gwen lest the fire burn his young limbs!"

Gwen instantly turned away and in a second had scooped up the child into her arms. Now she fixed her gaze on the baggage strapped to Glover's horse.

"What goods and finery hast thou brought here Master Glover?" she asked, swinging her hips in the provocative way she had done in their meeting on the road months ago. He looked at her fine strong body and the desire to take her as he had done then, raged within him. She sensed his desire immediately. Turning her back on Glover, she strolled over to a neighbouring home. As Gwen walked she held her head high, letting her long silky hair fall and tease the gathered skirts around her waist.

"Take the boy for a while Catrin, I beseech thee!" she called out to someone inside. A female form appeared and with a knowing expression, willingly accepted the child into her arms.

William Glover drew a plump orange from his knapsack and took it across to the beaming child.

"Slice this fruit into four quarters and let him suck on the flesh" he instructed, "in truth the juice is held to be good for the mind and body!" Fascinated by the almost perfect orange sphere the woman and child disappeared into the hovel. Turning abruptly Gwen fixed Glover with her eyes and moved towards him with the sleek satisfied grace of a creamery cat. He was weary, vulnerable and entranced.

Back inside, Gwen glanced around to ensure her patient was still sound asleep and then pulled a drape across the room, effectively screening this part from the living area.

William Glover knew that he was about to submit to his body's demands again and that he would regret it almost as soon as it was over. There was no way now to prevent the inevitable and once he was upon her, her soft round body cushioned and enveloped his in mutual longing. This coupling, however, was not the fast flaring animal passion that had ignited between them previously. The familiarity of the surroundings, the eye contact that they shared, the consideration for each other that underlay their passion, was new and different. She sighed with pleasure as together they rose and swam with the surge of lovemaking. When his excitement reached its peak, his teeth clenched and his head jerked back. Then he looked down at her and smiled, continuing his thrust until she too shared his pleasure. When they were ready, they rose together and in silence restored the room to its previous state. They worked in silence but there was a natural, comfortable calm between them. Still, thankfully, the patient slept.

Elizabeth opened her eyes very slowly and wondered if she was dead. Her last memory was of sipping a strange herbal mixture that blurred her brain and blazed in her belly.

Filled with terror and schooled by years of treachery, she feared that Gwen had given her poison. The last look of trust in the woman's eyes had comforted her and she had slipped into a slumber which had held her in its grip for more than twenty four hours. Again she was aware of someone at her side trickling liquid between her lips and over her tongue.

The aromatic fluid refreshed and soothed her throat; it was sweet and reminded her of her recent summer visit to Kenilworth. Memories of that magnificent new building for her handsome Lord Robert Dudley, of his dark good looks when he smiled at her and his outrageous presumption when he danced, made her heart throb for what might have been. She turned her head to look at William Glover.

"Is it done? Shall we be left in peace?" she asked, her eyes now closed again.

"Aye Madam, everything you asked is accounted for." Glover answered.

"Methinks thou art a worthy servant Will Glover" she said, barely moving her lips.

"Your Grace" he replied and putting down the spoon he had been using, he lifted her hand to his lips in reverence.

As he bowed his head The David Cross fell forward and Elizabeth was aware of its weight against her hand. Releasing his hold Glover drew the cross from around his neck and slipped it into her hand. Her slender fingers curled around it, exploring its shape and size. She lifted it close to her face and spoke through dry cracked lips:

"What manner of gift is this?"

"With God's blessing it will make thee well again" Will Glover promised and in his heart he truly felt that the power of the cross would heal the Queen. He felt at last that his actions were not in vain. He was glad to be free of The David Cross. Memories of the past had become a burden to him. It was time for the cross to heal and bring comfort; it should not bring despair and violence again. Once more the Queen slept and for most of the next day. When she awoke it was only to imbibe Gwen's new brew of marigolds, herbs, honey and orange juice. By the following day her improvement was noticeable.

"Send for the guards William" she commanded, "For we are rested and have had much time to consider our position. The Queen must return to her country. The people must have   their   Prince

Chapter Twenty

A Change Of Plan

Through the forest prowled the uneasy harbinger of change. Skies shifting from crisp azure to brooding purple-grey in an hour or two; enough to make the forest dwellers unsure of what the future might bring. Unsettled days between autumn and winter, that promised fair sunshine and then bit back with night frosts and cutting blasts of bitter cold.

The day began silently. A drab damp mist hung over the forest floor and gave a dream-like aspect to the forest commune. Spectre like, the trees bore witness to the events of that morning. They had no leaves left to rustle a whisper of alarm or to attract a young boy away from his fate. Gwen, William Glover and Elizabeth slept soundly after a busy day preparing for the Queen to travel back to Chepstow, this time accompanied by armed guards.

Gwen's son awoke early and his young mouth was dry and tasted bitter from the smoky air he had inhaled throughout the night. He remembered the succulent orange that William Glover had given him and wondered if there might be one more left in the knapsack. The boy's unsteady legs took him across the sleeping bodies and over to the entrance where bags were packed for the journey. He pulled on the heavy leather strap that covered the outside pocket of the knapsack. It was hard for his small fingers to undo but he could not ignore the possible delights the bulging bag. It promised fruit and the delicious trickle of orange on his parched tongue; he could not resist and was not disappointed.

His small hands held the prize for a moment before he punctured the over-ripe and browning peel with his thumbs.

Gwen opened her eyes and immediately searched the dim light for her son. Slowly she focused on his small body sitting by the door and holding something to his mouth. The recognisable fragrance of fresh orange filled her nostrils and she smiled:

"Wyt ti'n hoffi oren?" she enquired lovingly. "Do you like Orange?"

The boy looked round to face his mother. His mouth was wide open now; his face a mask of shock and horror. In an instant his pleasure had turned to pain as the juice trickled down his throat, burning with a searing bitterness that took his breath away. He gasped for air and then cried out as the poison from the orange hit his stomach and exploded with a force his young body could not bear. Still looking at his mother, the boy's gaze became lifeless and he fell forward. Gwen flung herself towards her son screaming his name, her heart gripped in a spasm of fear. William Glover sprang across the room and yanked the boy's lifeless body from the floor. He ran outside and held the child up by his feet, thinking that he must have choked and that there might yet be a chance to revive him.

"Jesu, let the boy down!" sobbed Gwen clawing at Glovers' arms until the blood ran across them.

"He can't get air!" yelled Glover now supporting the child across his knee and slapping his back.

"He is dead thou fiend of a man" cried Gwen and she snatched her child from him and pulled him to her chest.

Elizabeth Tudor emerged, her face pinched and grey she carried the remains of the orange in her hand and showed it to Glover.

"Look thee at this dark stain across the flesh" she said holding the fruit out to show Glover "the devil himself hath rose up out of the forest to poison the queen this morn!"

He moved towards her and took the fruit, examining it and then holding it to his nose. She lunged out and knocked it from his hand:

"Art thou mad that thou too wouldst drink the devil's brew?"

Gwen turned to face them both and her words were as bitter as the poisoned fruit:

"Damn thee that brings this evil to my boy and makes me

burn with grief!" the tears channelled down her brave face as she spat at them again: "I care not what manner of fancy lady thou hast brought to me but I would have her quit this place and ne'er cross my portal again!"

William Glover bent down and tried to encircle the dead boy and his distraught mother with his arms. She pushed him away and shrieked at them again, this time in Welsh. As he stood up, he was aware of faces all around him and he sensed their anger, their grief and their fear.

The soldiers from Chepstow were not due to escort the Queen until much later that day. Elizabeth had insisted that she be left hidden in the forest until she felt well enough to travel. She had thought herself safe amid the unknown forest, protected by ignorance and able to find the peace she craved. Albeit a few snatched days of escape from royal duty; Elizabeth felt in her heart that it might be the last time she would be able to make this kind of retreat.

It had been an opportunity to touch the lives of her subjects, to share the real world with them and to allow herself time to reflect and consider the future. She believed herself to be Queen because the people loved her. So she would eat black bread and pottage with them and learn about their lives. It was a brief education that no tutor could have given her and amongst them she felt out of harm's way. Who would ever believe that the daughter of bluff King Hal would live in a woodland community amongst potters, carpenters and weavers? Who would dare to imagine she was nursed by a whore and shared her days with a murderer? This was the unpredictable and sometimes outrageous way in which Elizabeth Tudor had outwitted her enemies in the past and would do so again in the future. It had worked and she had been given the precious rest and time that she needed to heal – until this day that is!

Now another attempt had been made on her life and the volatile forest dwellers were frightening in their grief. The safe atmosphere, which had nurtured her, was now transformed by raw emotion. Glover quickly went to find their horses and threw their baggage across the saddles.

"We dare not leave in this manner," protested the Queen to Glover.

"Madam we durst not stay lest they turn against us." answered Glover "Yet we shall return anon to make our peace with Gwen and the boy."

A protective ring of foresters comforted Gwen as they rode away that day. They did not even acknowledge the visitors' departure but debated the nature of the poison scornfully, some suggesting foxglove, others meadow saffron. Had they known that the poison was in fact a skilfully mixed combination of toxins, carried across the water and meant to kill the Queen of England, they might have handled the remains of the orange more carefully. The forest dwellers were not concerned for Elizabeth or any queen that day, nor should they be. They had lost one of their own and their hearts were united in grief.

William Glover and Elizabeth Tudor travelled out of the forest and onto the road. Across the valley lay the burnt-out ruin of Talbot Farm. They had been silent again; both reeling from the death of the child and the fact that when they had thought themselves secure, once again they were in jeopardy.

"Madam the gift of oranges came from a well-dressed man in Tintern" Glover explained. "I am so foolish to have taken them and put my trust in any man."

Elizabeth seemed resigned to her continued danger. She pulled on the reins of her steed and sighed heavily. Her stamina belied her frail body and pale countenance, but her distress was obvious.

"Sir, the life of the Queen is an abhorrence to many men here and abroad. Erstwhile thou served my father the King and for now thou art the Queen's bodyguard. We live under the threat of death each day. E'er long thou shalt be a free man again but Elizabeth will always live amidst conspiracy"

They sat together astride their horses and viewed the landscape before them.

William Glover was overcome with memories of the

Talbots and The David Cross. He turned to the Queen and surveyed her impressive profile; the slightly hooked nose, the princely way in which she held her head, her complexion that looked so fragile it might have been paper-thin. A complexion, however, that had mostly withstood the ravages of Smallpox. Such was the strength that underlay her whole being. She was a survivor. He was in awe of her.

"If I am to serve thee ma'am, then let me be a true servant and confess to thee my sins."

"Sins William Glover!" she mocked him and he coloured with shame and anger.

"The cross I gave to thee" he began "let me confess to thee the story of it that thou might give me ease in my soul."

She nodded and fell silent, realising he was in earnest. They started towards the Talbot Farm and as they rode, Glover told her the story, which had begun when her father King Henry V111 had ordered the sacking of Tintern Abbey. He pointed out the site of the overturned cart, the farmland and eventually faced with her the ruins of the farmhouse. At this point they dismounted and Glover completed his tale.

Elizabeth was not a good listener; she was used to being heard and having control over what was said. This story however, fascinated her because in Glover she saw a man of ambition, of great strength and courage. Yet also he was a man who was weakened by his emotions; just as she had been made vulnerable by her feelings for Robert Dudley. She saw a man who could have been her brother with his red-gold hair and bead-bright eyes; whose temperament matched hers but whose aspirations had been denied. She wondered what kind of man he would have been; given the scholarly education she had received and the power that was her birthright.

"William" she said, stretching out her tapered hand towards him "the Queen forgives thee and as God's own representative here on this earth I give thee good grace to be of sound heart. Thou hast made up for thy wrong-doing in saving thy sovereign." Their eyes met as he bent to kiss her hand but he knew full well that her words would not ease his conscience.

The Queen shivered and the shock of this new attempt on her life began to   break through the courageous countenance she had shown as they left the forest.

"Madam we should look for food and then rest before we return to the road and meet the guards." suggested Glover.

"Aye indeed" Elizabeth replied, "for these damned fevers and headaches that have gripped me of late are coursing through my veins."

"Mayhap thou art not ready for the......." began William Glover but the Queen snapped back at him:

"'Tis not the injury newly sustained sirrah! For years now we are plagued with bouts of ague and then the smallpox. 'Tis no wonder they fret and frown over the royal personage, lest they are left without an heir. Zounds but I am weary of this intrusion into the life of princes!"

The irritable outburst passed and her mood calmed. She looked at him in a pleading way that made him pity her sadness but envy her position nevertheless. She understood him.

"Wouldst thou trade thy life for mine William Glover?" she asked.

"Aye your Majesty I would."

"Wouldst thou live a life that brings conspirators to thy door each day?"

"Aye Madam I would." He met her gaze as he spoke.

Her voice fell to a whisper as their eyes met again.

"Dost thou not know it is not permitted to look directly into the eyes of the Queen William Glover?"

"Aye Madam" he answered, still holding her bright eyes with his own.

They were facing each other and although neither was aware of having moved, somehow they were but an arm's length apart.

"I am Elizabeth of England and it is God's will that hath brought me to this place William" she said, her voice very clear but still soft. "Would thou still change places with me knowing that thy life and thy body must be given for the people of the realm?"

"Is it too much for thee to bear?" asked William Glover "If it is then thou should stay here and we shall find a safe clearing in which thou couldst remain for ever in seclusion."

They were now so close that she could smell the male scent of his body despite layers of leather and woollen cloth. The wind blew a chill warning across her transparent cheeks and strands of Tudor gold escaped from her plaited hair.

"And should the Virgin Queen deny her inheritance, stay here and bed thee William Glover. Should the Lion cub bring forth young lions of her own?" she murmured as her breath warmed his lips.

"Aye Madam" William Glover replied, "if that is the Queen's wish."

"Is that what thou wouldst do?" she asked.

"Nay Madam," he said truthfully "I should never give up my right to the throne nor risk the crown my people have placed upon my head!"

She lifted her arms and placed her hands upon his shoulders, staring and searching his face, his head and his soul.

"Nor will this prince" said Elizabeth "but I will share this time with thee before I go back to my duty. 'Tis like seeing my face in a looking glass when I see thee William Glover. Thou art my mirror, my kindred, my echo."

The pressure on his shoulders was light but it was enough for William Glover to understand the intention of the Queen and to rejoice in his fate.

Leading her but still not daring to presume too much, they walked towards the Talbot barn, still intact despite the raging fire that had gutted the farmhouse. They tethered the horses and found a place in which to lie. William Glover was deliberately slow. This was not to be the frantic submission to his lust that was so often followed by remorse. Despite his instincts he ought to follow her but doubted that he could sustain a submissive role. This was to be the coming together of two people who were quite sure of their intentions and who were for a moment, equals in each other's eyes.

Elizabeth's body moved with the grace and precision of a feline predator. Her meagre appetite had allowed no surplus fat to distort the lean limbs or blemish the smooth white skin. Pale gold pigmentation freckled her back and chest as if she had been showered in fragments of gold leaf. The ivory flesh of her stomach was stretched across her hips like the skin of a drum and was exquisitely sensitive to his touch. As he lowered himself towards her, she raised her arms and wrapped them around him, guiding him closer and closer until their bodies were one.

William Glover watched the face of the Queen as he skilfully positioned himself above her. For a second her eyes closed but then she opened them not wanting to lose control. So alike were they in skin texture, hair colour and physical feature that the boundaries of their bodies blended and blurred as they became more closely entwined. As his ardour increased she pushed herself against him and was amazed that the rhythm they achieved seemed effortless to them both. He let his arm drop to support her back, remembering her recent injuries, and she smiled at his consideration. Still she remained in control, watching him eagerly, wanting to hold this memory in her mind forever. Aware of her scrutiny William bent to kiss her face. She turned away and immediately regretted her action. Raising herself slightly, she stretched upwards to his face and kissed him in a gentle almost questioning way. It was an innocent child-like kiss and he was moved by it. He brushed her neck with his lips and then allowed his tongue to trace a line down and across her shoulder. She sighed and pressed him closer to her again. At last Elizabeth traded her control for his passion. Together they moved with sweeping, interchanging flows of excitement and tenderness until at last they were fulfilled.

"God Bless thee Elizabeth" whispered William Glover in her ear when it was over.

"God Bless thee William Glover" replied the Queen and

her   eyes   burned   with   tears.

Chapter Twenty-One

A Life In Hiding

Sarah Talbot's hands were swollen and chapped so badly that her knuckles bled when she gripped the handles of the milk churns. In return for food and shelter she had agreed to work on the tiny dairy farm owned by the old couple that had carried them safely out of Bristol. It was turning out to be a miserable and exhausting way of life for which Sarah was ill suited.

The farmer was well pleased with the trio that fate had sent his way. The boy John, though sulky and quiet, was useful for gathering wood and helping to repair stonewalls. The girl, Bethan, seemed resigned to her lot and worked relentlessly cooking, cleaning, and churning butter. At first sight the farmer had decided to sell the boy's dog to a local sheep farmer, telling the boy that she had somehow lost her way. However after the first few weeks Tess was proving to have a real talent for catching rabbits and keeping down the rats, so at the moment it suited him to keep them all for as long as they wanted to stay, or until the food ran out. If the winter set in very cold then it was a struggle for survival and they would have no food to spare, no matter how useful the newcomers were to the aging couple.

The farmer's wife was less satisfied, mainly because of Sarah Talbot.

"They be a wondrous strange family, these three." She remarked to her husband when they first arrived.

"Aye" he agreed and then added, "They will say nought of whys and wherefores mark ye!"

Sarah continued to refuse to give any explanation of whom they were or from whence they had come, other than to say that a mishap had brought them to Bristol and that soon they hoped to have news from family or friends. No news came and the days slipped by.

"How does she think news will find her here?" asked the

farmer's wife one bitterly cold night. "'Twill be Christmas afore she knows where she is."

"Dost thou not want help around the place then wife?" shouted the farmer, tired of his wife's complaining voice. "Has thy aching back and swelling joints so much improved that thou canst manage the goats and cows thyself?"

"Nay husband" she retorted, "my back doth ache as much as ever and now my heart doth throb too; watching thy lecherous old eyes on that Sarah wench!"

"Thou art a foolish woman," the farmer answered.

He struggled to his feet; resentful at being driven away from the smouldering comfort of the log fire.

"Not so foolish that I don't see thee lusting after her plump breasts and her round belly!" said the wife, determined to have the last word. It was true of course. The farmer was not averse to mulling over in his mind just what this comely woman would be willing to do, in order to ensure food and shelter for her two young charges. It was obvious that she was not used to physical work and that the strain of it was breaking her spirit. He could bide his time and he would.

Meanwhile the three of them toiled each day from daybreak until it was too dark to continue. December came with winter clouds that shrouded the day. Long bleak nights stretched ahead, freezing the puddles of urine in the farmyard and making rock-hard trenches in the dung piled cowshed. John and Tess often went to the local blacksmith's forge, attracted by the blazing fire and sizzling white hot metal. John had first been there on an errand for the farmer, taking buckets to be mended and a pony to be shod. Now during the December afternoons he visited more frequently and began watching the Blacksmith and learning how he plied his trade. The farmer did not mind, it might be good to have the boy out of the way sometimes in the future.

Bethan always found chores to do indoors, she was used to hard work. For Mistress Talbot, however, life was fast becoming unbearable. They survived those first weeks by not speaking about the past or their feelings. Still in a measure of shock and exhausted by long working days, they were almost silent together when they retired for bed. John tried to blank out all memory of the past. Bethan lost herself in work as she had done many times before and at night slept deeply. Sarah Talbot numbed by the loss of her former life, humiliated by betrayal and fearsome for her future, went through the routine of sleeping and rising each day as if she were in a dream. Alone in her bed at night she wept silently. At first she had expected that they would be found and brought to trial for murder but when weeks passed and no visitors arrived at the farm, she let that fear drift to the back of her mind. She had no plans; she had no hope. Sarah was in despair.

A week before Christmas the farmer's wife sat stirring pottage by the fire. She threw in oats, turnips and sage; she was deep in thought. Her round face was tied up in a woollen bonnet that she had knitted many years before, when the swelling in her hands had allowed such craftwork. Now she was getting old, but not too old and although she was happy with young Bethan and grateful for the work she could do, Sarah was a different matter.

"I'll not have a new mistress here" she thought angrily "not by name or nature. I may be too old to give him sons but I can still warm his bed and see to his needs."

The flames of the fire leapt gold and amber casting shadows around the dwelling. Like the flames, ideas rose and fell in the old woman's mind. Some crackled and spat like the young green wood from the hedgerow. Then one sparked and smouldered and burned bright in her mind.

"Bethan" she called "is Sarah there with thee?"

Bethan scurried into the room and replied "Aye Madam that she be. We are darning for thee."

"Thank 'ee Bethan thou art a good girl." Praised the wife "Pray bid Sarah come and stir the pottage for me, for my poor arm is aching with the weight of this spoon."

Sarah entered the room. The farmer's wife had monitored the decline of this young woman over the weeks she had been with them. She was still lovely, her sweet face was delightfully pert and pretty, but whatever tormented her had left its mark. The farmer's wife had been fair to them all, but she needed to be rid of Sarah and a means of escape had occurred to this wily old woman. It could be a beneficial outcome for Sarah and herself.

Sarah took the great black spoon and stirred the vegetable stew obediently. The wife sat back in her chair and began to speak, letting her plan settle on the fire of possibility and then spark in the blaze of intent.

"Why Sarah 'tis nearly Christmas, we must get holly from the lower fields and trim the beams."

"Aye mistress" Sarah replied softly, not lifting her eyes and scarcely moving her lips.

"Methinks I am too weary to see the players in the village this year." The farmer's wife went on. There was no response from Sarah, whose gaze was beyond the smoking wood of the fire.

"Methinks I durst not venture to see the Christmas Players in the village this year. 'Tis a pity to miss the acrobats and jugglers mind. Dost thou enjoy the players Sarah?"

"Aye indeed mistress." Sarah eventually replied.

The farmer's wife watched as the pottage boiled and wanted to yell at Sarah to stir the wretched food properly before it burned, but she dare not spoil this opportunity.

"Aye Sarah, I love to see the players and there are pedlars too and songsters. How I shall miss going to see them this Christmas time."

The words were finally reaching Sarah and her eyes sparked with life for the first time in many weeks.

"In the village thou sayest mistress?" inquired Sarah.

The idea was smouldering and needed kindling just a little more.

"The village aye, not more than a mile from here" was the reply "and Oh Sarah, thou shouldst see the pretty ribbons and braids that they sell! Tell me girl wouldst thou go to the Christmas fayre for me and bring back some new lace and ribbons? Mayhap some wondrous fair trinkets to please an old woman; thou knowest enough to make the right choices."

Sarah eyes were alight as the prospect of escape from this dreary life revealed itself to her.

"I should be happy to go for thee" Sarah offered.

"Then thou shalt" promised the wife with relief "but we must be sure of the date for after the fayre they move on, taking the road to London."

"To London?" questioned Sarah, her eyes now aflame with anticipation.

"Through the towns and villages to Oxford, then London and away they go" said the wife enthusiastically. "Free as birds they be Sarah, away from the worries of the likes of us. A life of music and laughter and merry–making! 'Tis the life I should choose, were I a free woman I tell thee true!"

Enough had been said. Sarah's spirits rose seductively from the flames, so shrewdly fanned by the farmer's wife. There was no need for more debate and as Sarah left the room, the old woman settled back to her stirring. The good rich food bubbled in the pot and smelt delicious. Just below the surface, however, the stew had thickened and stuck to the sides. The flames danced around the pot prettily but the contents had been spoiled. The vegetables, once so fresh and nutritious, were burned black. When the farmer's wife dipped her spoon to the bottom of the pot she shook her head with disgust, for the food looked like charcoal and the taste was bitter as gall.

Part Four
New Beginnings

Chapter Twenty-Two

The Road To London

Sarah Talbot prepared to leave at daybreak before the farmer and his wife were awake. She crept into the kitchen where Bethan and John Talbot lay sleeping on straw pallets, as close to the fire as they dared. Her nervous stomach fluttered excitedly; her thoughts were in emotional turmoil. Once she had learnt of the opportunity to escape from the miserable and seemingly unfair lot that fate had dealt her, there was never any real debate in her mind. There were moments of guilt, of listening to her conscience, but they were fleeting. The decision to leave her stepson and their faithful servant Bethan with virtual strangers had not been easy to accept. She could see no way, however, in which she could take them with her. Sarah tried to convince herself that she would send for them once she had found a suitable home, but the likelihood of this seemed a distant dream. Dare she try to get back to Tenby and find again the loving security of her family? The risk of travelling west remained too great until the murder of Mark Fairbrother was long forgotten. Sarah had to get away and a group of travelling players would be excellent cover for a fugitive, until she reached London.

She wanted to wake Bethan to hug her and explain her reasons for deserting them. She did not have the courage. She wanted to kiss John's cheek and tell him not to be afraid for Bethan would take care of him. She did not have the audacity.

Sarah Talbot tiptoed out of the farmhouse with a few possessions she could carry. There was not much. The farmer's wife had left coins for Sarah wrapped in bit of rag and at first she hesitated to take them. Quickly her survival instincts made the decision for her. With every movement she thought "This is the last time I shall ever do this" and when she closed the heavy wooden door she felt as if she were shutting a door on the past. The fresh morning air made her shiver and her eyes glistened with tears as she made her way across the fields. There was no looking back however; there were no second thoughts. Sarah Talbot had relied on others for too long and they had consistently let her down. Now it was her time and she was determined to succeed. Bethan and John did not stir; Tess remained silent, cushioned at his master's side.

Only one person heard the low creak of the door as it opened, just wide enough to let a young woman slip through. Only one person listened as the worn metal latch clicked into place. She did not stir in her bed; she did not get up to look out and see the hurrying figure turn the bend in the lane. The farmer's wife smiled feeling sure Sarah would have seen the coins and taken them. That helped her conscience for she felt uneasy about manipulating Sarah. She had told no lies; she had just passed on information to resolve a problem concerning a clearly unhappy young woman and a husband who could not always be trusted. Feeling settled in her mind she eased the feather pillow around her grey plaits and stretched her flabby arm across her husband's belly. Now she was content.

By mid-morning the fayre was alive with visitors from hamlets and smallholdings around the village. Stalls were set up all around the village green and in one of the adjacent fields a small stage had been erected using bales of damp mildewed hay. The sound of raised voices, dogs barking, and bursts of music excited Sarah as she approached. Across the lanes the smell of wood fires and all manner of cooked food swirled and stimulated the taste buds of those who were tired and hungry. The farmer's wife had not exaggerated when she had described the fayre to Sarah; it was a delightful sight. Trays of ribbons, song sheets, sweetmeats, ointments and nosegays were among the items on offer as she neared the green. Every stallholder had his own cry or song to attract customers and there was a cheerful camaraderie between the buyers and sellers on that chilled winter morning.

The players, however, were a motley crew. They consisted of an adolescent boy, perhaps fifteen years old, who took the female part in the play, two much older men who were clearly bald beneath their wigs, and a jaundiced young man of about twenty-five who played any other parts that were needed in addition to some rather unsuccessful fire-eating.

Sarah was not impressed and her plan to join them and follow their artistic troupe to London, seemed in doubt. However she summoned up her determination and spent plenty of time around them, smiling encouragingly and putting into practice all her most endearing facial expressions and feminine mannerisms.

The evening brought renewed activity as those who had been forced to work during the day, now came with bulging pockets and expectancy in their eyes. Sarah was very tired and her eagerness sorely depleted. The players had now moved from their collapsing stage to the steps if an inn at the centre of the village and were enacting, for the third time that day, a play about heaven and hell and the devils of the underworld.

As Sarah watched the jeering laughing crowd around the actors, she spotted a covered wagon rumbling down the tracks towards the village. As it neared the inn her interest was aroused even further, for the pony that pulled it was trimmed with mistletoe and had ribbons plaited in his mane and tail. The wagon was covered in cloth of bright hues and holly was hanging in bunches along the side of its wooden rails. The players saw the wagon too and one whistled, waved and shouted across the twilight to whoever was holding the pony's reins. The light from the flares and fires around the fayre gave an amber glow to the December evening. It also enhanced the beauty of the woman driving the wagon, for her face blushed with a radiance that was remarkable. It made her stand out amongst the poverty-pinched faces of those around her. It made her look soft and comforting and warm. Her hair was long and fell in jet-black swirls around her shoulders and down her back. A crimson dress splashed colour across the night as she climbed down from the wagon and her black underkirtle was edged with lace and ribbon. She waved to the players and then patted the pony and left it to graze on the muddy grass, which had stubbornly survived the day's activity. The woman went into the inn and Sarah hurried after her, curious to see what she would do and what link she had to the players. The woman bought ale and food and then seated herself in a quiet corner of the inn.

Around her there was pandemonium; men and women were sprawled across tables and chairs in various stages of inebriation. Children were sitting, sleeping, crying, and crawling around the floor mostly unattended by parents who were determined to make the best of the day. Someone had vomited in the corner and a stray dog was lapping it up greedily. Sarah was reluctant to enter; all her instincts told her to turn back and return to the farm. She did not. Nervously she approached the woman:

"Good day" she said desperately.

The woman continued to eat, her eyes on the wooden trencher that held her food.

"Good day." she replied with a soft but disinterested voice. She paused and gently dabbed at the corners of her mouth with a bright yellow silk kerchief before continuing to slice the food with her knife. "I see thee watching me."

"Aye, forgive me I pray but I am in sore in need of a friend."

The woman stopped eating and looked up at Sarah. Her eyes were dark and her skin was lined, making her look older than she had seemed before. She studied Sarah for what seemed like several minutes.

"Art thou with child?" she asked bluntly.

"Nay!" said Sarah shocked "Nay, I am a widow woman and I need to travel to London."

"To London indeed," continued the woman "and thou wouldst travel with me in the wagon?"

"If thou wilt have me mistress." Sarah pleaded.

"I am not thy mistress" answered the woman harshly "I

am Rachel. The wagon belongs to the players. I travel with them for safety and I pay my way in kind. Thou should know that afore ye beg to come along with me."

Sarah's tired face was pitiful and Rachel understood her vulnerability.

She pushed the wooden platter across the table to where Sarah stood.

"Sit thee down and sup;" Rachel ordered "I will take thee anon if thou wilt labour alongside me."

"I will!" Sarah promised as she hungrily devoured the remaining scraps of food "I thank thee and swear not to cross thee or make trouble."

Rachel watched as Sarah Talbot swallowed the meat and gulped down the watery ale.

"Thou art a trusting soul," commented Rachel, taking in the details of the woman sitting opposite to her. "What is thy name?"

"Sarah T….." she hesitated and then decided; new life, new name. "Sarah Glover. I was married to William Glover, but he is dead of the smallpox and I am alone in the world."

Rachel recognised the rapid way in which Sarah had changed her surname but ignored it for the time being.

"Why dost thou put thy trust in a stranger Sarah Glover?" asked Rachel.

"Why madam, I have put my trust in men in the past and they have betrayed me every one. How could one of my own sex serve me worse?"

Rachel nodded in understanding and sympathy.

"I pay the players in kind Sarah." She repeated, watching a flash of anxiety cross the young woman's soft features. "I have need to return to London and in return for protection the men ……" now she looked straight into Sarah's liquid blue eyes "Dost thou understand my meaning?"

"I do. I have come to understand the ways of men and will do what I must."

The road to London was long but not arduous for Sarah. A close bond was forged between her and Rachel and together they served their travelling companions well. Sometimes they joined in the plays with songs and dancing and after every performance they collected money from the audience. The players soon realised that Sarah was a real asset. Her beauty attracted more men to the plays and Rachel was happier and more vibrant than she had previously been. They were a dynamic pair; one so dark and dramatically desirable, the other so fair and innocent looking with her full lips and flawless complexion. Between them they were an intoxicating combination of femininity, which drew men of all ages and sent them home from the fayres with lustful appetites. Rachel and Sarah quickly appreciated their newfound worth and began pocketing some of the coins heaped upon them by admirers. Some of it they secreted away, the rest they spent on themselves and on brandy. By keeping the player's bellies full of ale and brandy they were sure of an undisturbed night. The younger man and the fire-eater were more interested in bedding each other anyway. As for the other two players Sarah and Rachel were a godsend; they satisfied their egos, their stomachs and their lust.

On the road to London everyone was happy!

Chapter Twenty-Three

Return to Reality

As soon as the guards arrived to escort Elizabeth Tudor back to Chepstow and from there to Richmond Palace; the relationship between William Glover and the Queen of England reverted to that which their status decreed. Afterwards he could not remember her speaking to him, or even letting her princely gaze fall upon one so lowly as he, for the whole of the ride to Chepstow. The speed at which she was transported across the water to England was unprecedented. Fresh guards and fast horses awaited her arrival at every stage of the journey.

Sir William Cecil was beside himself with rage, anxiety and irritation. He had lied, schemed and risked his own head to protect this outrageous and foolhardy expedition. It had all gone dramatically and almost fatally wrong. If Lord Norfolk, Sussex or any of the other great nobles had discovered the true whereabouts of the Queen there could have been rebellion and anarchy. It was not the actions of a responsible monarch and in their most private moment of reunion he told her so. The Queen listened in silence. She could have had him arrested for such remarks but she chose not to. Instead she thanked him graciously and then pointed out that as she intended to give a lifetime of service to her country perhaps a few stolen days of privacy was not too much to ask. They both knew that she would never undertake such a perilous journey again.

Cecil went to speak but she silenced him by raising her hand and fixing him with her darkest stare. In a voice softened by emotion she said:

"We should not have grieved thee in this manner for all the world Sir William, nor should we have wished to put our people at risk. However, the Queen is safe and whatever stories thou hast spread to account for our absence we shall uphold. This has been a most important and eventful period in our life. We have been to the land of our forefathers and lived amongst the people. We have been at the point of death and seen others die. It is good for any wise Prince to do likewise if he wishes to understand and have the love of his people."

"My Liege........" he tried to speak but she silenced him again.

"If thou heed any man speak of this visit to Wales or of the attempts on our life, then he must be silenced. Fill all their pockets with gold but make sure that they never speak of this hereafter. Now, I prithee let us rest!"

She turned away from Cecil, knowing that yet again he would try to speak. He shrugged his shoulders in acceptance and walked to the door. When she thought he had resigned himself to dismissal, he called out to her:

"Madam my heart is full of joy to see thee and I am as ever your most loyal servant. God Bless thee."

"God Bless thee William........" she stopped herself short as the words she had exchanged with William Glover flooded into her memory and clamped her heart like a vice. Tears spilled over and trickled down the porcelain cheeks. In the privacy of her apartments with all her ladies banished till the morn, Elizabeth let the tide of exhaustion and remorse rack her body.

There would be a different Elizabeth in the morning. She would arise early; let them wash her with alkalised water perfumed with marjoram and clean her teeth with a mix of white wine and vinegar boiled with honey. They would chatter around her as she dressed in the dark, heavily scented Privy chamber. Then they would prepare with her the cosmetics; the lotion of egg white, alum, borax and talc to whiten her complexion and make her as pale as her beauteous cousin Lettuce Knollys. False veins would then be traced on her skin and the cheeks and lips blushed with vermilion. Her eyebrows, having quickly reverted to their natural shape during her time away, would be teased back into a fashionable sparse line. The auburn hair would be tightly curled at the front and arranged into rolls at the sides to support the jewellery and ornate head wear of the Queen's choice. It was an inevitable ritual and one that the Queen upheld willingly. With every application and adornment, Elizabeth Tudor would return to her role as Queen. This was the only way in which she would succeed in a man's world, where for so long she had been an unwanted heir to her father's throne. The freedom she had enjoyed in Wales was a luxury that had almost destroyed her. She had no regrets; she had lived and learned. Now she would rest and in the morning put on the royal mask and begin again the games of politics and intrigue.

For the first time in her royal apartments, the Queen undressed herself; it would be difficult to hide her injured leg from her ladies in waiting but she would try. The clothes she had travelled in would be burned; every link with the journey would be severed. Around her neck, however, hung The David Cross. She looked at it and thought of the man who had given it to her. She could not part with the cross; she must have something of him to remember. Elizabeth the woman had truly believed that Robert Dudley was the love of her life and that she could never feel such emotion for another man. This journey had proved that he she could love another. She had met a man so like herself in many ways that their bodies and spirits had come together in a way which overshadowed Dudley's self-centred coupling. She would always cherish Robert Dudley but a sea change had taken place and she could move on. Elizabeth Tudor climbed unaided into her royal bed and pulled the heavy coverlet over her frail body. She was thinner than ever, she seemed more delicate than ever, but that was the outward body of the Queen. Inside she was more formidable and stronger than before. Elizabeth's spirit was uplifted as she fingered the cross; she knew her role and was at peace with her destiny.

William Glover returned to Chepstow as part of the royal party. The leader of the guards formerly thanked him for his brave deeds and a bulging purse of gold coins was pressed into his hands. He refused it, letting it fall to the ground, his heart burning with indignation and disappointment.

Later that evening he sat alone in a tavern trying to come to terms with the events of the past few weeks. He felt angry with himself for refusing the coins, which he had real need of now his life was to return to normality. Suddenly one of the guards appeared in the tavern, handed him a letter and again offered the heavy bag of coins. He bent forward so that the taper burning on the tavern table would provide light enough for him to read. It was a poor glow and heavy shadows were cast across the paper. He read it over and over again that night and for many months ahead.

To Our Most Dutiful Servant William Glover

This letter comes to thee with our most heartfelt and true thanks for thy selfless duty to thy Queen. When thou art in receipt of this many miles of land and sea will already lie between us. Such is the speed with which they plan to restore the Queen to her people!

What hath passed between us over the past days must remain a secret betwixt God and ourselves. It is of greatest import that thy lips ne'er betray that which we have shared together. In truth we believe we might not have survived the past trials and perils were it not for thy courage and loyalty. Take then these coins for thou hast earned them. Rest in the knowledge that the love thou hast shown to thy Queen will be rewarded in heaven. God Bless thee William Glover.

Elizabeth R   *December   1566*

What more could he have expected? He knew in his heart that any contact with the Queen would always be strictly on her terms. William Glover could only be thankful and astounded by the events in his life, which had brought him into her royal presence. He did not contemplate the historical implications of what might have happened, had the assassins been successful.

William was overwhelmed by the events of the last weeks and could neither eat nor sleep without images and conversations blazing into his mind and setting his pulse racing. The implications of his actions tormented him. In the forest he had left Gwen and her community enraged and grief stricken; there had been no time as yet to return to her. He needed to thank her for all she had done, to share the gold coins with her and to sympathise with her over the death of her son.

Here in Chepstow he resolved to find Sarah Talbot and her charges and to escort them himself to Tenby if they had not gone there already. If she would allow him, he would like to make amends with Sarah and ensure the well-being of the youngsters.

For hours William Glover punished himself with visions of the fire at Talbot farm, the seduction of Sarah Talbot, the dying gasps of Gwen's son and the ferocious fights to save the life of a fugitive Queen. How much of this was his own doing and to what extent had fate intervened? It was an agonising but necessary time of reflection and self-examination for a man who had always been so self-assured and resolute.

The move to action came when he over-heard a conversation at the tavern.

Two seasoned sailors were discussing the high tides on their latest visit to Tenby and the passengers they had taken on the trip. William Glover decided to investigate the whereabouts of Sarah Talbot:

"Pray tell me good fellows, hast thou taken a young woman by the name of Talbot across to Tenby of late?"

The two men looked up and one grimaced:

"I have seen thee around these parts and thee breeds trouble."

"Nay not I" answered Glover "I fear for this woman's safety 'tis all!"

"Been no Talbots, lessen thou meanest the full-faced beauty with her childer and a dog." said the other man.

"Aye that I do." replied Glover excitedly "Hast thou taken them to Tenby long since?"

"We ain't taken them in the direction of Tenby at all half-wit" jeered the first "They be left for Bristol with young Fairbrother."

"Fairbrother!" exclaimed Glover yelling with surprise.

"Young Fairbrother aye, for the elder have died after some scuffle."

William Glover's mind raced trying to imagine what had made Mark Fairbrother seek out the Talbot family when his life was in danger for treason.

"How did he meet up with Sarah Talbot and why did they go to Bristol?" demanded Glover.

The first man whispered something in the ear of his friend and they both roared with laughter.

"God's blood man tell me what's afoot!" shouted Glover, his face now straining and pounding with blood.

"What's it worth to thee, master high and mighty?" sneered one of the men.

Glover dropped a coin in front of them; it hit the table and bounced to the floor. Neither man tried to retrieve it; they waited looking at Glover and smirking. Glover bent down and picked up the coin. They laughed again and one spat phlegm where the coin had lain.

The first man spoke at last:

"All I know is he was taking them all to Bristol. Said he had designs on the young 'un but would bed the Mistress and take what he could from her first. Said he would sell the boy on and keep the two women; put them to work for him with the sailors at the docks so he said."

"Thou liar!" cried out Glover and he leaned forward and struck the man across his mouth.

The man spat blood and ale across the tavern floor sending a cat that had been lurking under the table, scurrying across the tavern and out the door.

"Go see then!" shouted the second man "Get thee to Bristol and try the wench for thyself!"

Glover stormed from the tavern and went over to the castle walls. He looked across the water; it was black like a tar pool lapping against the rugged fortress.

"Sweet Jesus" he thought, "What further misery have I heaped upon this family?"

The two bibulous sailors were noisily helping each other

out of the tavern. They spotted the silhouette of Glover against the moonlight and yelled out again, taunting him:

"Get thee to Bristol and see for thyself!"

"That I shall!" Glover shouted back "That I shall and if I find Mark Fairbrother I shall kill him!"

Despair and dread overcame William Glover as he imagined the naïve threesome putting their trust in Mark Fairbrother. He had no doubt that what the men said was true for it was typical of the man. Leaning on the ancient wall his great strong hands cupped his face and he let his eyes close for a moment as the December night closed in around him.

A group of revellers passed, brimming with mulled wine and Christmas cheer. They called out to him but he did not hear them. Silence returned for a second and William Glover thought himself alone. He was not.

The two sailors, one still smarting from the blow to his mouth, returned to the sea wall. Fired with drink and vengeance they recognised an easy victim. Like starving curs, they smelled out Glover's weakened condition and sniffed at his heels hungrily. Overwrought by the physical and mental challenges of past events, he was easy prey if taken by surprise.

The attack was swift, one kicking Glover's legs from under him and the other grabbing his neck and pulling him backwards. The victim's head hit the cobbles with a deadly crack that rendered him unconscious at once. The two attackers, shocked at their success, kicked at Glover's ribcage sadistically until blood seeped through his wool shirt. One looked around nervously and whispered hoarsely:

"Enough, leave the bloody hot-head to die!"

His accomplice, mindful of his swollen lips, replied:

"Aye that I shall when I have cooled him off."

Standing astride William Glover, the man unbuttoned his breeches and withdrew his shrivelled penis. He held it out and let the acrid yellow urine fall onto Glover's face, who mercifully lay oblivious to this degradation.

"Leave it be," the other shouted "lest the watch catch thee!"

Reluctantly his friend agreed, putting an end to the torture.

The watch did discover Glover's pitiful body during his rounds and helped him to the safety of The Great Ship Inn. Glover had regained consciousness by that time and was slumped against the wall. He had felt for his bag of gold and unbelievably found it still in place. He knew then that he had been beaten deliberately and not as part of a robbery. He vowed to settle the score with the sailors anon. The injuries were considerable and kept Glover in Chepstow until the summer of the following year. Without Elizabeth's gold coinage he would not have been able to pay the innkeeper and would surely have starved on the streets of the old city. The blow to his head took a long time to heal and left a scar across his left temple. He developed pneumonia and on two occasions the innkeeper's wife left him for dead.

Each time he rallied she joked with him and urged him on:

"Thou art a teaser, Master Glover, with thy ramblings on! What an imagination thou hast! Talk of the Queen and oranges and fires a-burning!" she was spooning mutton broth to him and watching his lifeless eyes. He did not respond. When she had left he would take more coins from his secret bag and leave them for her, he did not trust anyone.

This was how the months slipped away until at last his health was restored. Three women dominated William Glover's thoughts. He had influenced their lives and the impact each had on him was great. Together they embraced all the desirable attributes of the female sex; individually they were still a powerful force.

Sarah Talbot had a gentle, voluptuous body and an air of innocence pervaded her lovely features. Like a sweetmeat she was tempting and delicious, a delight to savour and treasure. Underneath that cushioned surface, however was a selfish vanity that had been forged by experience into steely resolve. That was, as yet, for William Glover to discover.

Gwen was every inch a forest dweller, brought up part of

a special community whose lives were governed by the seasons. The skills and arts she had learned were centuries old, but her mind and body were vibrant and exciting like a seasoned instrument. She also had an underlying wisdom and tenderness shown in her love for her child and her compassion for others. She seemed in control of her destiny, but she was not.

Elizabeth Tudor was the pinnacle of many suitor's wildest ambition and her attributes surpassed all expectation. She was a force of mental and physical determination unmatched by those around her. Elizabeth overwhelmed William Glover as she did all men; she was unpredictable, fascinating, difficult and dangerous. However, she was the Queen and he was nothing.

Yet they shared an intense attraction that both accepted. Was it their physical similarity that pulled them together? Did they share an ancient ancestry rooted in the Welsh hills? Or had this been just a random encounter perhaps born out of temporary vulnerability and loneliness?

This was the state of turmoil in William Glover's mind as he fought his way back to health in 1567. He had unfinished business which had been delayed too long. He was finally ready   to   act.

Chapter Twenty-Four

The Search Begins

The summer of 1567 was unexceptional to most people in Chepstow; William Glover measured every day. He watched the Severn Sea warm to the glorious sun and bring with it treasures from east and west. He stretched himself on the grass and let the clouds shower him with rain or the noon sun scorch his face. It mattered little to him that the elements poured scorn on his body; he welcomed the ravages of nature seeing some kind of justice in his discomfort. When he did begin to fight back, when he did start to watch the changing moods of the summer days and seek shelter, he knew that he was growing stronger.

His first sojourn took him back to the forest in search of Gwen. She was the nearest and most accessible of the woman with whom he wished to make his peace. The woodland showed off to him in glorious shades of green. The trees let their verdant tresses rustle and shiver with anticipation as he rode along. The birds, frantic to carry the news of his arrival, darted from tree to tree and swooped gracefully through low branches before disappearing in the hedgerow.

William Glover was nervous; as he neared the dwellings and familiar work places of the forest community he dreaded the possibility of them being hostile. He was not sure how he would cope with violence after his last illness. He need not have worried for they greeted him warmly and remarked with genuine concern that he looked ill.

"Nay in truth I am much improved" Glover explained and went on to tell them of his experiences.

"Thou hast heard about Gwen I trust?" remarked one of the charcoal burners, surmising that she was the main purpose of Glover's visit.

"'Tis she I have come to see most of all and would have come sooner had I not been ...." He was unable to finish for they were eager to tell him the news.

"Why she hath taken off to London some six months since."

"To London?" Glover questioned.

"Aye, that friend of thine, yon sister or whatever, she hath sent a man-at-arms to fetch her. We thought thou had certain knowledge of it and must have left for London too." The man continued.

"Not I" answered Glover "but I prithee tell me more of the man that came."

They gave him refreshment, mutton pottage and dumplings, a rare treat in the forest. As they feasted the whole story was related, or as much of it as they were aware anyway.

As might have been expected, Gwen had been sorely grieved at the death of her son and the whole community had tried to help her come to terms with it. She declared that she could not remain in the forest and that she was to make her way to Chepstow, perhaps she intended to seek out William Glover. However, before that could take place a man-at-arms was espied on the Tintern road asking for the whereabouts of Gwen.

One of her sisters took up the story:

"Oh she was greatly relieved to be going, a real change came over her." the woman began. "She said that the woman she had nursed wished her to go to London and be in her service. She was sent wondrous outfits for the journey and gifts for us all."

The woman became pensive and sad saying:

"I miss her greatly Master Glover for she was dear to us all in her way. Her and the sweet child. Methinks Gwen saw it as a new beginning and thou durst not turn away from what fate sends thee, eh Master Glover?"

"Nay truly she was right to take her chance" murmured Glover, wondering why Elizabeth had taken this step and what Gwen's reaction was when she discovered the true identity of her patient.

"Is thy sister married to a wealthy merchant in London

William?" someone else queried.

"The lady is not my sister" answered Glover "but aye she will take good care of Gwen for she nothing lacks in goods and chattels."

He stayed the full day in the forest but left before dark. The memories of his time there were painful and weakened him again. He was relieved that Gwen was safe and well. Now he was free to find Sarah Talbot and perhaps to liberate her from the evil grip of Mark Fairbrother. He would need to be fit and well for that challenge and so he returned to Chepstow and waited another month before setting out to Bristol.

William decided to work his passage so that he could listen in to the conversation of the sailors and perhaps gain clues as to Sarah's whereabouts. The physical work was good for him, it made him breathe properly again, taking in great gulps of fresh September air. The vast billowing sails of the vessel he worked strained on the ropes and stretched Glover's muscles until they were flexible, lean and strong; just as they used to be. The rise and fall of the waves restored the strength in his legs as he fought to keep his balance on board the slippery deck. He was glad of it and felt himself growing stronger in every way. With this rejuvenation his determination and courage were also restored. His desire for vengeance and all thoughts of bitterness disappeared as he prepared himself for what was to come.

The sailors knew nothing of Sarah Talbot and when he mentioned the possibility of her being put to work in the docks, the enquiry was lost in a chorus of bawdy exchanges about past sexual encounters at Bristol and beyond.

When Bristol was reached Glover disembarked and walked slowly through the dock area, his eyes searching every painted face for one that was familiar. It was a fruitless errand and Glover did not know whether to be relieved that he had not found Sarah or worried even more by what could have happened over the past months. He had been sickened by the squalor and depravation he witnessed in the darkest parts of the city. Young boys and girls, men and women of all ages were offering themselves for all manner of abusive activity. Some were obviously diseased and undernourished; others were filthy with stinking mouths and discoloured teeth. Their faces reflected degradation and sometimes a despair that moved William in a way he had not experienced when he was younger. Being a fighting soldier with violence and death all around, he had created a mental barrier to protect his emotions. It was taking him some time to rediscover his human empathy; maybe he had never really cared much for others at all. The realities of growing up in the reign of King Henry V111 had made this young boy fearful, suspicious and focused upon survival.

"Surely Sarah and Bethan would not be forced to sell themselves alongside these poor creatures?" thought Glover.

He found a lodging at the very top of a three-storey timber framed house that had been squeezed in amongst a row of others just as tall and narrow. For the next three days he scoured the streets, watching, listening, asking anyone if they had heard or seen Sarah Talbot and the children. Many ignored him; some mocked his accent which now had a distinctly Welsh lilt. It was only when he visited the wool market that he found success. Fixed to a stall was a crumpled piece of paper on which someone had drawn a man's face. It was smudged by the daily business of the stall and weathered by months of rain and sunshine. It was one of several such portraits, mostly of men. Clearly, however, the artist had done his job well. The face that stared back at William Glover was that of Mark Fairbrother.

William struck up a conversation with the market trader, enquiring about the price of a woollen vest. This done he moved swiftly to seek out information. The news again was shocking and left Glover speechless:

"Dost thou know the man then?" asked the trader. Glover nodded.

"'Tis said he was in his cups on the boat" the trader went on "travelled across from Wales or some such. Art thou from that area?" Glover nodded again.

"Methinks he had a surfeit of ale," the trader continued "and lost his footing on the cobble steps. Banged his head when he fell and died that instant. 'Tis not the first time them steps hath sent a man off to meet his maker!"

William Glover found his voice:

"Pray was the man alone?" The trader shrugged his shoulders:

"Nobody seen a-weeping for him." He added, "His picture hath been here for nigh on six month and thou art the first to ask. Art thou kin?"

"Nay, we worked the boats together sometimes 'tis all."

The trader tore down the picture and handed it to Glover saying:

"Here thou canst have the likeness."

"Thank 'ee no sir" answered Glover "Thou art most kind but 'tis not mine by rights."

The trader called out as William Glover turned to walk away:

"What manner of man was he? Thou hast not spoken his name!"

"Mark Fairbrother" Glover called back over his shoulder "His name was Mark Fairbrother!"

Relief flooded through Glover but was quickly chased by frustration. He had no clues as to the whereabouts of Sarah, Bethan and John Talbot but at least he knew they were not under the control of Fairbrother. For another two months Glover stayed in Bristol, searching for the trio every day and praying that fate would somehow bring them together. It did not.

Resigning himself to the fact that they had probably worked their way to Tenby and were safely in the home of Sarah's parents, Glover abandoned his quest.

Should he now go back to Wales and on to Tenby? The alternative was to remain on English soil and follow Gwen's footsteps to London. The notion that he might somehow be able to see Gwen and Elizabeth again teased his mind and would not let him escape. There was no real doubt in his mind; he must go forward and seek out the two women.

Sarah Talbot would have to wait.

Chapter Twenty-Five

The Bankside Geese

The fates, however, would not let Will Glover have his way. Over the years he had been allowed glimpses of what might be in store for him, only to be thwarted and denied. Like a baited bear he had been teased and sported with by destiny, sometimes lashing out cruelly and inflicting pain on others in his disappointment. If fortune had a grand plan for Glover he was being made to work for it and each step of the way was fraught with surprise and heartache.

The journey to London was bleak, lasting weeks and taking Glover and his horse through terrain that was difficult even in good weather conditions. Heavy rain had left the roads impassable in places and many carts and coaches were badly damaged. For safety Glover travelled in company whenever he could, joining groups of merchants, farmers, and gypsies for some stretches of the journey. Whenever he could he spent the night at an inn or tavern, making sure, like all good soldiers, that his horse was fed and well-shod and his own belly was lined with wholesome food. Many times, as he sat watching the innkeeper's fire leap like a dancing thing, he thought of Elizabeth Tudor. He tried to picture her face in his mind, but somehow he could not fill in the details of her features. There were days when he wondered if he had dreamed it all, perchance he had been enchanted by forest sprites and he was mad. The reality was there, however, evident in Gwen's life and deep within his heart. Was he right in making this pilgrimage? Without her gold coins, he could not have financed the journey; somehow he knew he was where he should be.

Less than five miles outside London, Glover's horse became lame. The poor creature stumbled on a jagged boulder on the roadside, lost a shoe and was thus unfit to ride. A brightly covered wagon was approaching Glover, travelling in the opposite direction. Two men sat at the front chatting as their horse negotiated the mud and stones with an experienced trot.

"Pray sirs," called out Glover waving to them "Pray sirs rest awhile I prithee!"

The wagon pulled off the road onto some dry turf where the Glover was standing.

"What's amiss?" asked one of the men rubbing his chin suspiciously. They were right to be on their guard on this dangerous highway.

"Fear not sirs" Glover replied "'Tis a smithy I have need of."

"What business brings thee to London?" asked the second man, studying Glover's solid frame and good quality clothing.

"I am come thus far to seek out an acquaintance and mayhap find work."

Gambling that Glover would not prove to be a dangerous companion the first man suggested:

"Follow us if it please thee. Our destination be but a small town to the north of this road. 'Tis a short ride and the smithy there be a good man."

Will Glover tied his horse to the back of the wagon and jumped up alongside the men. They were good company and Glover was grateful for their help and their lively conversation.

"Art thou a married man?" Asked one of the men when there was a lull in the conversation.

"Nay, in truth I have never married." Answered Glover.

"Pray what is thy name good sir, for surely thou art a stranger on the London Road?"

Something made William Glover hesitate, but he had no reason to withhold his identity and so did not. The two men shared a look of recognition, nodded and then looked back at Will.

"Methinks I know that name" said one thoughtfully "but never wed ye say?"

"Aye sirs in truth I am unmarried." He smiled and was mystified "What meanest thou with these looks and nods?"

"'Tis nought but a wench we knew of late, she was one Sarah Glover. Claimed to be the widow of William Glover," the man remarked.

William Glover listened intently, his thoughts racing nervously.

"Joined the troupe for a while she did," continued the first man, "able to do all sorts one way and another!"

The man nudged his friend and they laughed uproariously together.

"What manner of woman was she?" ventured Glover.

"She was a beauty right enough!" one responded, "Her face was like a child's so pink and pretty! Little fair curls and cheeks for pinching. I tell thee Master Glover I should have liked to have had her for myself, but she would belong to no man again she said."

Will Glover's incredulity turned into astonishment as the men went on to describe Sarah Talbot so vividly.

"I tell thee what I miss since she hath been gone; that be the lovely perfume of her soft white flesh." mused one dreamily.

"Aye indeed she seemeth like a flower, always scented with lavender and honeysuckle."

"Roses thou dolt!" argued his friend mockingly "Little bags she had with rose petals and lavender heads."

William Glover's wits reeled as he remembered the fragrance of this lovely woman. He plucked forth memories that he had denied for many months. Again he enjoyed the sweet visions of Sarah Talbot in his mind's eye. He recalled the first time he had visited the Talbot farm and caught her making lavender bags. He recollected the intimacy they had shared at Chepstow; the touch of her fine downy skin, the sweetness of her breath and always the enchanting essence of lavender and rose.

The players were masters in the art of mime and body language. They had no need to question Will Glover further; his every expression and gesture told them the truth.

"Where might I find her?" asked Glover.

"She hath gone to find her fortune with the players in London," offered one man.

"Aye get thee to the inns and play-yards and seek her out" encouraged the other; "mayhap thou shalt find her in the company of Rachel, a dark-haired beauty."

Glover had his horse shod, paid the innkeeper for the players to feast upon 'the ordinary' (meat stew thickened with vegetables and bread) and then bade them farewell.

This chance encounter had raised many questions in Will Glover's mind: what had happened to bring Sarah into the company of the group of players? Where were Bethan and John Talbot? Why had she gone to find work at the plays when young boys acted out all female parts? The players became increasingly vague in their responses to Glover's questions, as the amount of ale they consumed increased. He could wait no longer to be back on the road and so left them while they were still jovial and thirstily guzzling the innkeeper's ale.

"Ask for the Bankside Geese!" one shouted as he left the inn.

"What need have I of geese?" replied Glover laughing at their drunken nonsense.

"Aye in faith Will Glover" repeated another, "Find thy way to Southwark and look for the Bankside Geese!"

Will Glover shrugged his shoulder in confusion and delivered himself into the hands of fate.

Groups of travelling players had wandered the byways of England for centuries, calling at towns and villages to entertain and then move on. Increasingly, however, groups of players were staying in London and performing their dramas at semi-permanent sites. Often the plays were held in the courtyards of inns and hostelries, where patrons could be entertained, as they made merry. There was increasing rivalry between groups of players as rich takings were there for those with enterprise, especially when visiting merchants arrived in the city. Occasionally players were asked to perform in private apartments, even those of the Queen, and then the rewards were even higher.

William Glover made his way towards Southwark, having found one notorious inn yard to be so full of expectant revellers that members of the audience were being seriously crushed and injured. He marvelled at the number of people bent on entertainment that October afternoon. He had tasted the varied enticements of London many times over the years. The restless pulse of the city never ceased to excite and surprise him.

Open to the elements except for a draped canopy of scarlet and gold, a makeshift theatre had been set up in the courtyard adjacent to an inn. The inn itself was called "The Merry Drop" a name that seemed dedicated to the spirit of the crowd. The innkeeper obviously profited well from the plays and was improving the yard over time to cater for the growing number of customers. The floor of the yard was a mixture of crushed hazelnut shells and mud. In some parts Glover could see straw too and he suspected that bull's blood might have been put in the mix, as the deep crimson surface was hard and shiny in parts.

Every element of London society seemed to be making its way to the play; laughing, teasing, pulling and shoving in an excited way, which cut across class and status. Once inside the yard, the wealthier part of the audience seated themselves on wooden benches set up at different levels in an almost circular formation. Many more stood at ground level and were elbowing each other for space. A very unstable-looking stage had also been erected and a curtain hung somewhat precariously behind it. This was the cramped area where the actors were trying to prepare themselves. There was much shouting; calling out of orders for drinks and food and outbursts of laughter or jeering. Young boys scurried between the crowd, ducking the elbows and fists that jerked and jostled, carrying mugs and platters of fare.

William Glover's experienced eyes scanned and searched the crowd for a glimpse of Sarah Talbot. The play began but she was nowhere to be seen. He looked up at the rolling grey clouds which bullied each other across the sky. They threatened rain before long and another fruitless excursion for Glover.

The crowd roared its approval as the first act ended; William had been so preoccupied that he had no notion what enjoyment he had missed. Several people around him took this opportunity to move around, some going inside the inn, others waving to friends and calling out to each other. A short round-bellied man moved closer to Glover and spoke some words, which were lost in the clamour of the audience. Fumbling in his breeches, the man then proceeded to urinate on the floor, splashing Glover's boots and making him jump back in alarm.

"God's blood man!" swore William Glover losing his balance for a moment. In this theatre of society the basest needs of men were acknowledged and accepted. As he turned to regain his footing a group of musicians disclosed themselves and their gentle tune floated like birdsong across the yard. The audience began to calm and turned expectantly as further movement in the crowd was made. Between the throng several female figures seemed to be drifting and the people were making way for them. They were dressed in white and as they drew closer, William Glover could see that they were heavily made up in courtly fashion. One of the women wore a titian coloured wig; another had jet black curls piled high upon her head. Their skin was white as a goose egg and glazed so shell-like that it seemed it must crack and splinter. They moved with a confident undulating gait, their eyes searching the crowd as they neared the benches where the more affluent spectators were to be found.

The murmur of the crowd increased gradually as they passed and sometimes their vermilion lips pursed and teased the onlookers with smiles and whispers. Glover watched them, fascinated by their presence.

"What manner of player is this?" he asked his neighbour, whose face was now florid and sweating liberally.

"They be the Geese" was the reply "and they be making

for the merchants' purses."

William Glover watched as the two women, still accompanied by the lilting notes of the musicians, arrived amongst their quarry, flapping their long white sleeves and skirts so that they were easily seen from any distance. Finally they nestled down on the seats which were made ready for them. The music ceased and two jugglers acrobated into view, met by squeals of nervous delight as the audience saw the unsteady stage rock dangerously. Still Glover could not take his eyes from the blanch-faced women who now preened and prepared themselves before their own audience of appreciative men.

The red-haired woman raised herself from her seat and seemed to be engaged in heated discussion with one of the foreign merchants. He raised his hands in frustration and waved a bag of coins at her, at the same time shouting in a foreign tongue. Several of the crowd yelled at him to be quiet and the woman hissed back an oath as she turned to move away.

Thinking better of it, the merchant grabbed the woman's arm and pulled her to him. She let herself fall towards him so that she was almost sprawled across his lap. He began to laugh and shoved the bag of coins down the front of her bodice. Now she smiled too and turning to face him, sat astride his ample gut.

The play began again; the black-haired goose had also secured a customer and was now busy at her work. Supported by the inn wall she pleasured her customer, her white-stockinged legs gripped around his waist, his head jerking back rhythmically as he thrust himself inside her. After some initial curiosity, most of the crowd lost interest in this coupling and allowed themselves to be thrilled and amazed by the outcome of the plot.

The titian goose, having satisfied the foreign merchant, had now moved on to his companion. Glover had seen enough. And yet the realisation had not dawned on Glover. His quick brain, dulled by fatigue and a surfeit of new experiences, had not recalled the words of his recent companions:

"Find thy way to Southwark and look for the Bankside Geese!"

The woman in the wig was approaching William Glover. She held a nosegay to the lower part of her face, a popular device thought to ward off the evil-smelling humours associated with plague. The man at his side nudged him and smirked:

"Look to thy private parts, the Geese are coming!"

"Oh Jesu" Glover whispered to himself "Oh sweet Jesus no!" he shuddered as his ignorance melted away.

The face moved towards him; his eyes held hers. The scarlet slash of mouth parted to reveal yellowed decaying teeth. This was not the perfect smile of the woman he sought.

"Thank God" breathed Glover as she passed him. It was not Sarah Talbot. The relief was too much to bear and he bent forward, retching on the bulls-blood floor. His relief, however, was to be short-lived.

October 24th 1567. Years later William Glover still remembered the date, which was unlike him for he had never been a keeper of dates and diaries. He overheard two merchants mention it as they wearily departed from the inn-yard; some transaction, some trade or trickery they had agreed upon on this day.

The rain clouds, after much posturing and deceit, finally precipitated upon the array of tousled heads in the yard. It refreshed some intoxicated fools and damped down the spirits of others. William Glover merged with those heading out of the courtyard in the direction of London Bridge. It was early evening and he had left the players frantically covering their costumes to ensure that they were dry for the next performance.

He was following the Bankside Geese. The ladies in white had worked throughout the second and final acts of the play and now, having paid their dues to the innkeeper, were also making for the bridge. There were four of them that afternoon, none of whom, on closer inspection could be mistaken for Sarah Talbot. They remained, however, the only tenuous link that Glover had, so he continued keeping a close but secret watch on the dark-haired woman. The women moved quite swiftly towards the bridge and from thence to a tall narrow house, the ground floor of which was a baker shop. They entered through a back door and mounted a flight of narrow wooden stairs.

"'Tis only we four Master Richard," called out one of them to the Baker.

"Aye" he responded good humouredly "I reckoned 'twas thee or the fishmonger."

The dark-haired woman darted back in the shop, picked up a lump of dough from the oven tray and threw it at the baker. He shouted out and dodged back laughing.

"'Zounds Rachel thou art a damned hussy!" the Baker bawled, scraping the sticky dough from the plaster wall of his shop.

Just outside William Glover witnessed the scene, at the same time savouring the reassuring smell of fresh hot bread. The woman's name was Rachel! The puzzle was beginning to fit together at last. There was no way that Glover could ignore this information if he really wished to see Sarah Talbot again and to make his peace with her. His heart told him that his future could lay with this woman and that in some way he could repair the damage of the past.

He climbed the stairs and knocked the small wooden door. As it swung open, a delicious floral fragrance wafted towards Glover.

Sarah Talbot's bright round face was clearly recognisable despite the fashionable eggshell façade with which she tried to mask her identity.

She did not appear to be shocked or surprised, nothing it seemed could touch her now.

"Sarah!" gasped Glover.

"What ill wind brings thee to my door?" she replied coldly.

"I must speak with thee" Glover began, "I have searched

for thee and the children. Pray let me come in and ..."

"Nay Sir, hold fast." Sarah broke in abruptly "If thou wouldst spend time with me then wait at the inn on the bridge. Be sure to bring thy money mind, Master William, for the likes of me don't come for nothing these days."

"Sarah" repeated Glover, a desperate pleading in his voice. His hand reached out to her arm but she shoved him away. "Wilt thou not let me make good the harm I have done? Can I not make provision for thee and the children?"

"No man shall ever betray me again William Glover!" her voice had fallen to a whisper now and her eyes burned with vengeance:

"I would have the life of a whore and let men grovel at my feet rather than take a new master!"

"Thou speakest in anger Sarah" Glover entreated "Forgive me I pray thee, let me restore thee safely to thy home."

"Thinkest thou that I should ever return to be a farmer's wife, or a serving girl or even a bedfellow for the likes of thee?" She tossed her pretty head in agitation; angry sobs shook her voice but the tears would not flow. Her hands gripped the door securely as she said:

"I choose to be mistress of my own life and when I have enough gold in my pockets mayhap I shall return to Wales."

She paused and looked beyond him as she spoke. She did not trust herself to deny the overpowering combination of his vibrant manhood and his ardent speech. It took all her strength to declare:

"Indeed, I was finished with men when I sent Mark Fairbrother to his death. Now I just sport with them."

She watched his expression as the impact of her words stung like a slap across his face. He knew that her cold dispassionate statement hid a deep unhealed wound.

Once more William tried to intervene:

"I beseech thee Sarah turn away from this life of danger and disease!"

Sarah's self-discipline was fragile and so her response had to be final:

"I do not want thee William Glover, not thee nor anything that thou could offer me. I am unsure of the true manner of my husband's death and could not rest suspecting thee as I do. What chance would two murderers have together? I can only look to myself and pray that I will survive. The children are safe at Burbage Farm, five miles east of Bristol. Now I bid thee farewell."

She closed the door and despite the furious banging of Glover's fists and his pleas for her to meet him again, the door   remained   shut.

Chapter Twenty-Six

A New Life

William Glover found rejection hard to stomach. He was a man whose need of women had been readily satisfied and he had always been the one to turn away from responsibility and commitment. The confidence which married with pride to make the man, could not at first believe that Sarah Talbot would prefer the degrading life of a harlot - no matter what fancy names the crowds had given the women. On several occasions he made his way to the plays but although Rachel was often in evidence, Sarah was not to be found.

Winter was ready to seize the city; already the River Thames was biting cold. The wind was blowing hard from the east, making the ferryboats dither and the barges splash icy waves against the riverbank. The River had a will of its own. Some days it brought a foul stench and fetid vapours, especially in the summer months when excrement and rubbish were flung heedlessly into its shadowy waters. At this time of year it could freeze over, bringing the river traffic to a standstill. As the freezing temperatures dropped in January and February, the ice was sometimes solid enough to hold markets and fayres on the river. William Glover had never witnessed this and was tempted to stay. A decision had to be made. His options were not great; should he remain in London for the winter, for the year, for ever? His life seemed to have lost its purpose. When he had given away The David Cross, he had passed with it his ambition and his hopes for the future.

Perhaps he should remain in London and rebuild his life near to the only woman who had ever really understood him. The one who over a brief period in time had looked into his face and recognised a kindred spirit. The one he did not have to explain his feelings to or put into words the thoughts in his head. William Glover and Elizabeth Tudor had met and, for a moment in time, shared the peace that comes when one soul acknowledges its mate.

Once he had allowed the memory of the Queen to fill his mind once more, the only decision he could make was to stay and see her again. He smiled to himself and thought with self-mockery:

"For 'tis so very easy for a common man to meet with his Queen! Thou art a dolt Will Glover and a foolhardy vagrant to even consider it!"

The possibility of just glimpsing Elizabeth Tudor again, was the kind of difficult challenge that was needed to give Glover a reason to carry on. This was the sort of dangerous plan that he loved; just like the young Will Glover had galloped away from Tintern in search of The David Cross and again when he arrived in Bristol to seek out Sarah Talbot. It could be done – if you had the will and determination to succeed.

There was a way of course; one which had presented itself to him at the plays. Since he had been in London he had learnt much about the thespian activities in this city. The groups of players were competitive and fights often broke out between rivals. The innkeepers demanded a high standard of performance to draw bigger crowds and gradually the business of the theatre was developing. There was money to be made: refreshments, seating, covering for the inn-yards in wet weather, crowd control, finding new venues, maybe even becoming an actor himself. The industry was in its infancy and mostly because of the need for a permanent place to perform the plays. If the gentry, or even royalty, wished to see a play it was difficult and dangerous for them to visit the inns. This being the case, the players would take their art to the Great Halls and Palaces at the invitation of the owner. This is where William Glover might have a chance; if he could somehow involve himself with a group of players and join them when they performed at the request of the Queen.

It took him until Christmas to achieve his aim. The players hired a barge to take their costumes and props down river to Hampton Court where they were to perform. William Glover was there to fetch and carry, lift and lever, haul and generally help out. It did not matter to him what he did, just as long as he could get access to Elizabeth and to see her eyes when they met his. He was supremely confident that the fates would intervene again. He was confident, arrogant and unprepared for the future.

In the royal apartments, the maidservants moved swiftly around the Queen, attending to her needs. Her wide-skirted dress of purple silk and satin was spread out on the bed in readiness. The bodice was heavily embroidered with golden thread and decorated with pearls. Her shoes were made of fine calf leather and also trimmed with pearls, they had been dyed pale lavender and matched her silk stockings. The dress was newly sewn; the Queen had ordered several dresses to be made this last six months owing to a slight increase in weight. Everyone at court had been delighted that the Queen seemed happier, more relaxed and had begun to eat more. Her temper was less vicious and she seemed, William Cecil concluded, more at peace with herself and resigned to her duties. As the clothes were laid out for Elizabeth the scent of woodruff, a haunting, fresh, nutty fragrance, lingered in the room. All her bed linen had been packed neatly in great carved chests using leaves of dried woodruff between the layers, just as the Queen commanded. The distinctive bouquet gave her pleasure and created an atmosphere of serenity.

William Cecil was relieved. In Elizabeth he saw a healthier Queen who had promised to wed and would surely now fulfil her destiny. The future of the most powerful men in England remained with this Tudor Prince and they would rise against her still, if they sensed that she was weak. This most astute of advisors watched and waited for her to need him again.

Elizabeth stood, arms outstretched, and allowed herself to be robed. At her side constantly was a new member of the household, a woman who had somehow won the Queen's confidence and was always in attendance. The other ladies mistrusted and were jealous of the newcomer, especially when she had given birth to a child recently. The Queen had discovered, it seemed, that the woman's husband had been killed when he tried to control a startled horse in the royal entourage. The Queen had taken pity on the woman, it was said, and vowed to help her and the child. This swarthy-skinned female arrived with a royal escort and was immediately taken to the queen's private apartments. Those who witnessed her arrival were appalled at the common manner of the stranger. Their response had been anticipated and changes to the new arrival's appearance were immediately put in place.

Gwen had settled uneasily at first. The ladies were suspicious and envious of her familiarity with the Queen. They dare not question or be seen to harbour resentment, however, for they all lived in fear of Elizabeth Tudor. For some it was welcome relief that they no longer had to suffer their mistress's ugly moods for long periods. The swearing and violent outbursts they were privy to in the past could be terrifying and unpredictable. They dreaded that they would return. As Gwen's pregnancy became more obvious, they warmed to her and were genuinely concerned when she complained of bouts of sickness or swollen legs. They watched as the swelling belly seemed to increase steadily over the months. They fussed whenever they could, offering remedies of herbs and salves. Gwen knew better than to disclose her own knowledge of such matters and tried to accept their kindness graciously. They sometimes laughed with her, begging her to speak Welsh for them. When she did they squealed and shrieked so stupidly that it always brought an irate Elizabeth into their company. The Queen understood, however, the need for her new maidservant to become part of the household. She tolerated the frivolous tittering, therefore, which in the past she would have cursed.

When the baby was due to be born, Elizabeth prepared a special room in the royal apartments next to her own, and would let only a trusted midwife be there for the lying-in. It was the custom that when an expectant mother's time was due, she take to her bed and await the birth, after which there would be a period of bed rest. Many women died in childbirth or just after; infection was rife and childbed fever widespread even in royal circles.

However, this was not the way of the forest-dwellers and having prepared ancient brews of her own making, Gwen was still heard pacing her apartment during the time of labour. There was no bed rest either and within hours of the birth the mother was back on her feet and, although weak, ready to resume her duties within hours.

Elizabeth involved herself devotedly during the first weeks. This was not so unusual as she openly enjoyed the company of children and cared greatly for the well-being of her most trusted ladies. It was a unique and very private time. The child was strong and cried stubbornly when her needs were not met. She was, mused Gwen wistfully, the image of her   father.

Chapter Twenty-Seven

An Unexpected Audience

In the great Kitchen at Hampton Court a magnificent fire roared and spit boys sweated wearily. Heavy black rods and chains strained to lift and turn the roasting joints of meat. Grease spat and trickled, skin crusted and split as the flames licked greedily at the royal fare.

The stone floors, scuffed with the aged footprints of King Henry's time, were known to twist and snap a kitchen maid's slight ankle. They walked therefore, fearing to run, but their gait was hasty and purposeful. The solid walls, blackened in parts from smoking furnaces, reverberated with the sounds of the kitchen and its workers. It was a tense, demanding, ruthless place to be when the Queen was in residence.

The demand for food was continual and the retinue of consumers seemed to increase every year. It was a wondrous place, however, for those willing and able to tolerate the hard work. The great wooden tables displayed all manner of grey-green herbs from near and far. There were spices in pots and jars that hinted at secrets and mysteries the sailing ships had only glimpsed. At this time of year, the kitchens were garlanded with evergreens. The swirling loops of shiny green embraced the arches and portals of the old Palace and enriched it with earthy forest freshness. It was a period of thanksgiving, of celebration and ancient customs. It was a magical time when the old ways bowed and gave up their lifeblood so that the new might prosper and flourish.

William Glover followed the players along the cobbled passages that skirted the servant's halls. He peeped in at the kitchens and larders, stole a look at the pantries and cold rooms where preoccupied workers barely glanced at the passing entourage. His stomach churned and fluttered in response to the delicious sights and smells from the kitchens, but also from his nervous anticipation and uncertainty. The preparations for the play were long and arduous; the actors fractious and unreasonable. There was much cursing and jealousy; on one occasion Glover's arm was bitten in a skirmish between two rivals. They had waited three hours, when all was finally ready, for the court to present themselves and request the entertainment to begin.

The quest to see the Queen was futile. Glover was kept well out of view and bombarded by demands from the players. Sycophants continually surrounded the Queen herself; security was high and the play itself over quickly. Afterwards the business of packing up the costumes, scenery and props began. This was not of interest to Glover; the players were no longer of any significance to him. This was his chance to be near to Elizabeth again and even if he were arrested for treason, he would not be denied.

Glover broke away from his companions and retraced his steps through the kitchens. Exhausted servants were now leaving their posts for the day or else languishing around the fires contentedly, enjoying a lull in the demand for victuals. Some sipped mulled wine and let themselves slip into inebriation, others heartily swallowed ale and shared rumour or court gossip. Another strange face meant little to them and there was something about William Glover's smile and familiar tone that made them comfortable and accepting of his presence.

"Is there room by the fire for a man to warm his hands?" he asked courteously.

"Indeed there is sirrah" replied a greasy-aproned cook. "Wilt thou join us for a posset?"

The company seated around the blazing logs stirred briefly and someone pointed to a spit-stool that was vacant by the hob. Glover smiled and sat amongst them. The dancing flames lit the burnished gold in his hair and he seemed young again.

"Nay thank 'ee," William Glover responded politely. He leant forward, holding his hands like a priest before the altar of the fire. The penetrating heat stung the blisters and cuts his hands had suffered while moving the effects for the play. He knew they watched him, so he waited a while before venturing:

"Dost thou know if the amusement is done with this night?"

"Bless thee no!" answered the cook, dipping her hand into a bowl of raisins. She tilted back her head and stuffed them into her mouth greedily. Still chewing them she spoke again, pleased to air her knowledge of the Queen's arrangements.

"There be fireworks at midnight down by the river, and fires will be lit by Her Majesty to burn away the evils of the old year and light up the way for the new. 'Tis a most wondrous sight to behold!"

William Glover offered his thanks and hurried out of the palace and across the lawns to the river. Crowds were already gathering around the bonfire and music could be heard getting louder as a procession formed at the palace gates. A jester led the way, his tunic of red and yellow stripes illuminated by torches that lined the path. He carried a stick on which was a small model of a man's head. He was singing a bawdy song about King Phillip of Spain and every now and then he made suggestive movements with the stick. The more crudely he behaved, the more the crowd laughed uproariously.

Suddenly the Queen was there.

"Yon fool is more foolhardy than the one he sports with!" she joked.

"Indeed Your Majesty" added a royal companion "methinks he will singe his wit in the fire, if the Spanish ambassador is in earshot!"

The moonlight gleamed a flattering light upon Elizabeth's white face. It made her seem ethereal; her skin like fragile silver-leaf. He had forgotten how powerful she was and how her presence dominated all around her. He had never seen her before amongst her court and magnificent though she was in courtly attire, she had been equally commanding in forest garb. Her voice was light and yet it had a quality and passion that set her above all around her. Surrounded by great nobles, aristocratic court beauties and gaudily dressed toadies, there was none who matched her grace and supremacy. Her purple dress had a high semi-circular collar that fanned out behind her neck. It was made of silver lace and decorated with stars; some auburn strands of hair were tangled in it behind her neck. He was close enough to see this, even in torchlight, and to yearn to stretch out and free the hairs that ensnared her. A move towards her would probably have meant instant death, but he was determined that she should see him. He looked carefully at the bonfire and watched her moving towards it. If he could manoeuvre himself into a position directly opposite to her when she lit the fire, then surely she would see him in the firelight. It was a chance, but then their story had always been about chance and fate and the power of the spirit.

Elizabeth Tudor was happy; she was enjoying a brief period in her life that would never be repeated. Only she knew the turmoil in her heart as she bent to take the torch to the fire. The sparks blew dangerously as the timber caught alight and there was much snapping and spitting as the twigs and branches burnt. She straightened her back and withdrew from the flames just as the first firework showered gold and silver across the black night. Her eyes looked up and her mouth opened slightly with delight. He was directly opposite and in that split second he called out her name:

"Elizabeth, Elizabeth Tudor!"

Their eyes met and merged. She lurched forward slightly and a small gasp escaped from her lips. Someone caught her elbow and steadied her. It was a woman, who was instantly at her side and who supported the Queen as she swayed. It was Gwen. The Queen turned and moved away swiftly leading the revellers away from the bonfire and back towards the palace gate. The fireworks continued, the Queen regained her control and the incident passed unnoticed. Elizabeth, however was in shock; she trembled, she shivered, she ached.

"Methinks the cold will kill this goodly Prince!" she said to her retinue at last "Come let us return to the comfort of the

Great Hall!"

The party moved back into the Palace, save for one, who had an errand to perform. William Glover knew the answer to his questions; he had seen the Queen's eyes and read the emotion in her soul. The firework that lit the sky when they saw each other might well have been a shooting star, for the fates were riding on that night and their spirits were fused in the glow. He waited for the message that would surely come. Gwen was the carrier of that message and when he saw her approach he blazed with excitement. The change in Gwen was remarkable. The dignity with which she carried herself, the way in which she spoke and copied the courtly gestures of her peers seemed almost comical to William Glover. He knew better than to give a hint of this humour. His joy at seeing her again and in such fortunate surroundings was genuine. He moved to greet her enthusiastically but she kept her distance.

"Gwen thou art much changed! I am so pleased...."

"Me changed!" Gwen snapped back, "thou art greyer and wiser I trust! Follow closely and keep thy silence!" she commanded. "Thou hast been granted an audience with the Queen."

He did so, with no knowledge of the news that was to greet him or of the way in which his life would change.

Chapter Twenty-Eight

A Game Of Cards

The sound of Gwen's feet on the tiled walkways and stone stairs that snaked in and around the palace, stayed with Glover forever. He remembered lucidly the events of the night when he had followed her obediently, to a meeting with the Queen. He recalled the sound of fireworks exploding across the river and the taste of the fire on his lips. His agile body had slipped in and out of the shadows; his senses acutely aware of his surroundings. If the nervous energy that he exuded had been lit like a flame, he would have burned with a dazzling halo of golden light.

Elizabeth awaited his arrival in a secret chamber hung with the ancient tapestries her father had imported for his private pleasure. The tension in the room was almost unbearable. He emerged from behind one of the tapestries; once Gwen had opened the panelled door for him she had tactfully returned to the royal apartments. William Glover fell on one knee and kissed the hand Elizabeth extended to him. He dared not look at her and stayed with his head bowed low. She stooped towards him slightly with his lips still on her hand. With her other hand she gently stroked the auburn hair, which nestled at his neck. Even in candlelight she observed the flecks of grey and remembered fleetingly the difference in their ages. She felt him shudder in response to her touch. She spoke his name and drew his head towards her so that the pressure of his lips on her skin intensified. His leather jerkin was stretched across his back; she breathed in its animal scent that mixed with the man and the fire. Reluctantly she withdrew her hand from his kiss and tilted his chin so that he could gaze upon her majesty.

"William Glover" she said softly, her eyes darting over his face with undisguised pleasure, "what sport thou dost have with thy Queen. We thought 'twas a devil in the fire when we beheld thy dear face!"

"No devil madam, but thy humble servant!" he replied.

She stepped back so that he might rise to his feet. At last they faced each other again.

"Comest thou in search of Gwen?" Elizabeth asked after a moment's silence.

"Nay, well……. aye madam. I have looked to make amends with Gwen but they told me in the forest that thou hast brought her to thy court."

He spoke jerkily, aware that she scrutinised his every move, feature and word. She had the ability to see deep into his soul and yet she asked him questions that seemed superfluous.

"I have suffered greatly in spirit since we parted and have tried in vain to make good the wrong I caused for all parties."

She smiled and tilted her head in a quizzical, almost mocking way:

"Thou hast come here to seek out Gwen or to see thy prince?"

"Prithee do not mock thy servant" he retorted bravely "thou knowest full well that I am here for thee Elizabeth Tudor."

Her mood changed instantly again and she lowered her eyes, looking tired and overcome with emotion.

"Tell me all," she said leading him to a couch, "let me hear it all from thy lips before we give thee our news."

For almost an hour he related the events that had brought him to her side. She listened intently, sometimes touching his hand or laughing with him as he described some of the characters he had met. It was an interlude that flowed like a river; chattering excitedly over shallow stones, sometimes leaping over rocks with shouts of outrage and curses, only to plunge occasionally to deep pools of emotion and soul-searching.

When he had told it all, she paused before beginning her story. She felt like a player in a game of cards. She held all the aces and yet was bound to lose. There must be measured amounts of honesty and bluff if either player was to survive the game. The decisions she had considered over the past months must now be decided upon for the good of all concerned.

The woman or the Queen? The friend or the rival? The lover or the benefactor? These were the choices. Elizabeth's heart dare not rule her head – the lessons had been hard to learn.

"'Zounds what a life thou dost lead when thy Queen is not there for thee to protect Will Glover!" as she spoke, feigning a detached cheerful air, he prepared himself for the worst.

He knew at once that he had lost the game of hearts and that she would send him away. He bowed his head so that his eyes could not watch her perform this painful dismissal.

He understood the pain that tore at her heart as she silently explained to him, pleading with her eyes:

"Please understand why I must do this and do not hate me for it. If the world were changed and thee a prince or I a pauper, then we should be together and nothing on this earth would part us."

The words she said aloud were those of the Queen:

"William we owe our life to thee and to Gwen. We wished to reward thee and to give thee thy freedom to build a new life. For Gwen, however, there seemed to be no clear way forward. She was alone and desolate in her grief. 'Tis for that reason that we sent for her and let thee go William."

Glover went to speak but she raised her finger to silence him and let it touch his head in a caress that was almost a blessing.

Elizabeth continued:

"She came to her Queen as a loyal and trusted friend. God knows that we have need of that! She came that we might support and protect each other; she was to be our eyes and ears. She was to be like my dearest Kat Ashley.

There was a pause in which Elizabeth reached for his hand and held it in a firm grip that was forged with passion.

"Then…" she stopped once more and he read the anguish in her face "and then we discovered that she was with child

William. She was full-bellied with thy child!"

It was done! She had told him her news and the shock had been as tumultuous as she had predicted, coursing through his body and into hers as she held him. She felt the danger, the risks and any future for their relationship fly up into the air like a pack of cards and then cascade down upon them both.

Elizabeth's eyes searched his bemused features trying to read and answer his questions before he could pose them.

"Gwen hath brought forth a daughter William, a most beautiful child who hath thine hair and eyes and temperament." She turned so that he would not see the tears that slipped over the shiny glaze that masked her face.

"Gwen hath a child to be eyes and ears for; we would not take her from her motherly duties. 'Twould be too selfish especially now that the child's father hath shown himself."

The dialogue seemed unnatural and painful, underpinned with deceit and despair.

"Well William, now thou canst see that any plans we might have shared must be forsaken for the sake of our dear Gwen and thy most lovely daughter."

William Glover had prepared himself for the possibility of life changing fortunes when he had engineered this meeting. He had never for one moment considered that this would be the outcome.

"Think on all these things William and we shall meet again this morrow. Thou shalt remain here this night; there is food and drink prepared for thee. Do not show thyself 'til then."

She left the room swiftly, allowing only the sound of the closing latch to confirm her departure. He remained alone with his thoughts throughout the restless night.

"Sweet Jesus!" William Glover swore, "How the fates do make fools of all men and their princes!"

Chapter Twenty-Nine

The Will Of The Queen

Three weeks after the meeting between William Glover and Elizabeth Tudor, a very private wedding was held in the chapel at Hampton Court. It was a place of ghosts as past memories merged with the future hopes of those kneeling before the altar. The wisps and strands of long-forgotten blessings and prayers hovered on the beams of light that sneaked their way defiantly into the chapel on that winter's afternoon.

William Glover had never looked nobler or more gracious. His physical presence dominated the women that surrounded him and from behind Elizabeth looked at him and thought, not for the first time, of her father. Elizabeth chose to wear a relatively subdued outfit of Tudor green. She was trimmed with acorn-coloured suede and muffled with ermine against the blasts of cold air that blew around the palace. Gwen was allowed to be the centre of attention for the duration of the wedding ceremony, dressed in a gown of gold brocade and a cloak of wine velvet, she was truly remarkable.

The child was christened immediately after the ceremony. The holy water trickled icily over the translucent skin of the child. She cried lustily in protest and shook the wisps of Tudor-gold hair that framed her cherub features. Elizabeth was her Godmother and chose the name with which she was baptised. She was holding the child as the priest gave her the name Anne Elizabeth. She looked lovingly into the child's innocent face and then up at the face of William Glover, whom she knew would be watching her. For an instant they both thought of what might have been.

It was a strange union; there had been little dialogue between the bride and groom since his arrival. They had been alone only twice in the past few days and then just briefly when they were too exhausted or too afraid to speak meaningfully. Once Elizabeth had made her decision, plans were put into place quickly and there was little room for discussion.

"Pray do not think that the Queen acts without understanding of thy feelings," she had said to them both "I have spoken with Gwen many hours and more, William. I am sure that thy marriage will give thee and thy child a life that is good and full of love. A child needs to grow in a safe home where she can run free."

"What of thee madam?" Gwen had asked.

"God's blood, fret not for thy Queen. The people must have their prince and they shalt have that in this Tudor Queen."

Too much had passed between the three, for them to be convinced by this bluff response.

Elizabeth realised their misgivings and changed her tone. She held out her hands, one for Gwen and the other for William Glover. She spoke truly from the heart this time:

"Fear not for Elizabeth. I am of sterner stuff than most, fashioned from a true King and anointed by God. We shall amuse ourselves with the Archduke Charles and dally with the French Frog. Handsome courtiers will enrich the court and entertain our days. Only God knows if we shall find a Prince worthy of our love. For now I am resigned to be the Virgin Queen, for that it seems, is the only way in which I can uphold the power of the throne."

Gwen's fingers clutched at the royal hand for the last time:

"Art thou sure there is no place in thy life for a husband and a child?"

"Those are gifts for thee to enjoy" was the Queen's reply "and while thou art at home with thy family, thy Queen shall make merry at the royal court."

She smiled, but almost instantly her face changed and she looked fearful and grave.

"There will be difficulties, even warfare mayhap and ever those who would kill to replace me"

"Madam I would stay with thee and serve thee if it were thy will!" Gwen persisted.

The Queen glanced at her affectionately and replied:

"The court is no place for a child Gwen. Much as it would please us to have thee at our side we must be brave enough to release thee. God hath shown his hand by sending William Glover to us; that he might claim his daughter and take her to safety."

The generosity of the Queen was boundless. The weather suddenly turned mild and during that brief respite from winter the new family returned home to Wales. They were escorted across country and then by sea back to Chepstow.

The child flourished, although a wet nurse had been employed for the journey as Gwen's breast milk had dried up following a fever just after the wedding. At the request of the Queen they stayed in property owned by William Morgan of Monmouthshire while their future was decided. They had much to discuss and consider, for their lives had changed dramatically in the passing of a few months.

The speed with which the Queen had married and despatched the couple was alarming. William Glover seemed resigned and detached from the proceedings, Gwen was uncharacteristically tamed and compliant; so very different from the woman he had known. It was a strange and unnatural alliance. This was a marriage blest with a child out of wedlock and it seemed then that there would be no more children. Neither William nor Gwen wished to consummate their marriage and slept together awkwardly, like brother and sister. It was a bizarre turn in the relationship which had begun with physical passion which both had once craved. They were good friends, they were fast becoming good parents, but they were not lovers.

Doubts burned in Glover's brain. There was no question that the child was his, had she followed Gwen's colouring he might have questioned the paternity, knowing Gwen as he did. But this was not the case; her skin colouring, bright eyes and auburn hair were identical to his; his and Elizabeth's. Therein lay the doubts that tortured him and held him night after night. If there had been no child would there have been a chance for them to be together still?

William Glover tormented himself with her words:

".............now thou canst see that any plans we might have shared must be forsaken for the sake of our dear Gwen and thy most lovely daughter."

Did she mean that? Or was it a convenient way in which to rid herself of an embarrassing relationship which must never become public knowledge? The Tudor court was full of rumour, whispers and gossip. She had said as much on several occasions. If she had not married Robert Dudley she would certainly never risk bringing William Glover to court, no matter how she dressed him up and showered him with goods and land. It would have been impossible and they had always known that. A whore, an old soldier bedded in a moment of weakness and their bastard child, were not fit company for a queen. William Glover must accept the situation and be realistic and responsible. Elizabeth could afford to trust no-one. He understood that. Yet he recalled her face when they parted. Recognised again the choking in her voice as she bade them farewell. Saw the reluctance with which she handed the sleeping baby to Gwen. Overheard once more her whisper:

"Guard her with thy life sweet sister and know full well that our heart goes with thee!"

Then she had turned to him and her mask of kingship had fallen, showing him the woman's face that he had known erstwhile.

"This is God's will and we must bear it. God bless thee William Glover."

She was resigned and he dare not question the will of the Queen.

"God Bless thee Elizabeth." He had replied, before turning away from her. His face was stone grey and his heart weighed   heavy.

Part Five
Of Lavender and Rose

Chapter Thirty

Gwen's Story

I take up the story now lest thou should think that my part in all of this was that of a bystander or a foolhardy strumpet. In faith I have been these things and more and yet as I reach the end of my years I am proud to have been Gwen Glover.

They are both dead now; the Queen and my William – and he was mine though thou might think that his heart was always with Elizabeth. The Queen, God Bless her, passed over last year in March 1603. My William hath been gone this ten year or more at Easter, dying in his sleep aged 71, which is a goodly age for a man.

He would lie down in the bed, thou knowest, and I was sore afraid that if he did not sleep sitting up the angel of death would find him.

"Pray, William, my love" I beseeched him "Let thy pillows be plumped at thy back so that thou canst sit upright and cheat the angel of death."

But he did laugh at me and sometimes curse me for my ways. 'Tis no matter, in truth he had outlived all his fellows and none could remember a time when William Glover had not been master in these parts. None but me that is, or those who had heard tales and rumours but forgotten the gist of them over time. I weep for Master Glover now and shall do 'til I see his handsome face again in heaven where I truly believe him to be. He was my husband for over twenty-five years and a good father he made, despite the strange turns it all took for me to win him. Methinks it were all God's will that we should find each other and have our dear family. Neither him nor I desired marriage, yet we were both the better for it.

Dost thou believe that I married William Glover to please

the Queen or for the sake of Anne Elizabeth? Nay look to the story and recall that I raised my first dear son alone and would have raised Anne without a man if it had been God's will to do so. I desired William Glover the first time I saw him in the forest and willed that he should come upon me blackberry picking on the road. He was meant to be with me for I had seen it in the cards and felt the yearning in my soul. When he brought Elizabeth to me I was sure our fates were sealed. I could have killed her when she was at my mercy, as she thought I might, but I soon could see that she was no threat to me, for all her clever ways. They were as one and any numbskull might see that. But it could not be in all the world, men and fortune would never let them be together. They were too close, like kith and kin not lovers. That is the way it is with the fates sometimes and we mortals must abide by it.

It was early 1568 when we began our journey home. The Queen's mind was full of the troubles in Scotland. She was glad, she said to have matters of state to take her thoughts from our leaving. The Queen was a prudent woman; I had heard her before we left ranting and swearing at her ministers, threatening war on Scotland. No one knew the secrets hidden in her heart. She had turned away from Elizabeth the woman and chosen the power of a Queen. It was her destiny.

William and I returned to Wales worse than strangers, he could not look at the child or me, without me reading the grief in his eyes. For my part, I ached for my husband and longed for him. I waited; I held it in my breast and bided my time. She understood, the Queen, my conspirator and my friend. We shared so much in heart and mind that she knew I was strong enough to wait for him. We had the child and she understood that we would love and cherish her as long as we both should live.

We stayed in William Morgan's house for two years while the old Talbot Farm was rebuilt for us. The Queen provided everything in those years and I had a nurse for Anne Elizabeth who taught me to read and write. Quite the lady I became after my spell at court! To aid my education, I began writing a diary of day-to-day events as the weeks of Anne's childhood slipped away.

Elizabeth, as Anne's Godmother, wrote to us quite often and as time went on I found courage to write back to her and give her our news. She sent gifts to Anne Elizabeth and even sent an artist to make a likeness of the child. Pray let me tell thee the rest through my diary and letters for then thou shalt have a true account and can follow the years with me. William never wanted to read the work, though he had always boasted of his reading skills. He would listen, when I gave him news from the Queen, but it hurt him and I understood. He built his life for us and that was the only way in which he could live.

I shall find thee extracts from the pages that thou might see the way things worked out. Forgive the errors, I prithee, for my writing skills cannot match those of Anne or either of the boys. 'Tis a joy to me that I have ever learnt these devices, for all expected me to live the life of a whore and die of the pox at 30 years of age! If my eyes did not fail me now I should be writing still and not dictating this for someone else to scribe. Trust me then I pray and thou shalt hear what came to   pass.

Chapter Thirty-One

Measuring The Days

Letter from Queen Elizabeth to Gwen Glover

2nd December 1569

My Dear Gwen who art a true servant and goodly friend,

Greetings from thy Prince and good wishes for Christmas. We know not where the court will celebrate the birth of our Saviour for we are torn with unrest and uprisings. Richmond is my warm place, but Greenwich may be safer. We are much eased that thou art safe in Wales for the rebellions in the North are a great threat to our people. There is much blood shed in the name of religion and thou knowest that it is not what we desire, for enough hath been spilt in our sister's reign. Fear not, however, that we shall resolve the issue and make an example of all the traitors who dare to shake the throne of Elizabeth Tudor.

Tell me of the child I beseech thee, for I conjure her in my mind's eye each night afore slumber. Monies will be sent to thee for further building on the Talbot house, it must be a fit home for the godchild of the Queen. Also prithee take these rolls of velvet to make her gowns anon and the jewelled combs for her hair. There is finest silk for thee too and books for Anne's nurse. For William, plans and advice on the farm chimneys and the leaded glass for the windows.

God Bless thee Gwen   *Elizabeth R*

Gwen's Diary: My very first entry 1st October 1570

I write this day as we are at last in our new home. William wished us to be removed for Anne's third birthday but alas there was trouble with the roof and I know not what else. 'Tis the grandest of houses and seems to me called a farmhouse in jest; for indeed there is no place it's equal in all the county to my knowing.

Diary: 2nd November 1570

We are to have visitors this Sabbath. My husband hath been away these last ten days. He traversed to Bristol and then to a dairy farm. Methought he was seeking knowledge for the

farm, but no, he hath found the children John Talbot and

Bethan. He hath been sore agitated of late but now seems content that they will come to the farm.

The rain hath fallen unceasing this month and we needs must build a bigger barn for the milk herd afore the snows.

Anne Elizabeth hath a temper I care not to cross. Indeed she drives the nurse to curse and swear under her breath. William says we must have a tutor for the child as she is beyond the nurse's understanding of letters and such. She hath done me proud as thou canst see. I wrote to the Queen today and am feared that she will make sport with my letter. I care not for she be many miles from the farm and her brain must be addled with all the troubles up North.

Diary: 23rd December 1570

John Talbot and Bethan the maidservant are an odd pair. He do limp and scowl and she, though most beauteous fair, hath the cares of the world on her young shoulders. There hath been a fearsome spat betwixt William and myself, for I thought it could do no good to bring young John back to their old home.

"Care thee nought for the boy's feelings?" I bawled at him. William Glover is a proud man but he will have his way. We have sworn oaths and cursed each other but he would not be shifted.

"The boy must see the land and know that I would do right by him!" he yelled back at me and I saw the purple veins beating in his temple. It maketh me love him all the more when I see his blood is roused, but I dare not move towards him still.

There is a bitter wind from the East and the fields are thick with heavy clods that make outside work to no avail. Thank God I am no longer in the forest.

Diary: 28th December 1570

Little Anne rejoiced in the gifts sent by the Queen for Christmas. I have received a letter from Thomasina, one of the Queen's ladies, who remembers me at court and wishes to keep correspondence now that I am able to write. (She did not know of my ignorance afore but the Queen hath confided in her as to our whereabouts.)

The Talbot Farm, for William insists that the name remain unchanged, was a wondrous sight at Christmas. We had a bonfire in the upper field and old friends from the forest came and danced in the Great Barn. I never saw such drinking and feasting since I left the court, but William would have it to thank them for the past.

I was ill at ease for time hath changed Gwen Glover. Methinks some of the men were looking at me with their thoughts full of past times in the forest. They would never believe that my marriage bed remains unstained after all this time. I grieve to think of it myself. I am content despite that. When I see the forest dwellers now I would not change their world for mine. I pressed William not to bid them come again and he nodded, as he does.

John Talbot hath scorned William's offer of land and a place at the farm. He hath trained as an apprentice with the smithy who serves the Burbage Farm in England and declares that he be not willing to farm. Marry, he is not able-bodied enough in my mind! It maketh my teeth bleed the way he do sneer at my William.

<u>Diary: 5th June 1571</u>

The Queen hath sent me a small likeness of Her Gracious Majesty wearing a six-stringed loop of pearls. She doth inform us both that the necklace belonged to her cousin Mary from Scotland, the one who doth still grieve the Queen so sorely. It is to be passed to Anne at some time in the future, but for now she durst not part with it for it is known to so many at court.

The Queen hath become enamoured of a dark, handsome Gentleman of the Privy Chamber. His name is Christopher Hatton and she reports that he gives her much pleasure.

She warns against gossip and confided in her letter:

"We can tell thee naught in games of love Gwen. If William is our golden sun, then he is but the silver moon – a pale reflection of what I have known. There can be no future in it so heed it not! Yet it is the way of princes to seem to make idle sport while in truth we watch and listen to the murmurs of the court. If Leicester was our eyes, then Hatton is our lids; such are the needs of the Queen if she is to rule her court."

The Queen is a mighty clever woman.

Diary: 29th August 1571

June and July burned stifling hot and scorched the mouldy roots in the soil bed. The seed soaked and mildewed by the wet spring, hath mostly given up the ghost. The farm hath suffered a poor harvest and William hath bought shares in the Wireworks at Tintern on the advice of the Queen. She warns that we must protect ourselves against the fits of the weather and invest money for the future.

William is such a handsome gentleman now I cannot bear to be apart from him. Indeed, with his growing interest in the Wireworks, I fear that he will seek the comforts of the women of Tintern. I am resolved to win him to my bed, for he is my husband and I have born my patience bravely. I'faith 'tis not Gwen's nature to let a man deny his needs!

'Tis many a month since I called upon my wise-woman ways. On the morrow I shall hasten to the banks of the Wye and gather the herbs and bark that I need to brew a love potion.

Diary: 30th August 1571

Mayhap the power of fate hath intervened in our lives again this day, for reader, I have no need of my potion. He came upon me as he had that day in the forest; I about the business of harvesting fresh herbs and he travelling along the Tintern Road. He said he saw me instantly and believed that the spirits of the field were playing tricks with him, transporting him back in time to that moment of our first love making.

I laughed to myself and was in wonder that he still doth not see the workings our fate. He was all the bold angry soldier again; riding me with a fiery lust that overcame us both. I played the strumpet, gasping and sighing, full of fervent release. He was fast spent the first time and lay almost in shock at the side of me for a while. There was no need for us to waste our time with prattle or remorse. I led him into the woodland and found a cave I had once known as a child. It was to be our lair for the next few hours.

My husband's body hath ever been a delight to me; his skin hath a clean manly smell to it that doth set my heart racing. When we are coupling he holds my eyes with his and watches me rise to meet his passion. I pleasure him in all the ways I have learnt over the years and have him quivering at my touch. I am proud that I have this power over him, for it is a spell that is safe with me. I should never abuse or cuckold this man, loving him as I do.

We are become ourselves again and have returned to our home united, with no Queen nor child nor memories between us. I pray God that this miracle will last.

Letter to Her Majesty Queen Elizabeth 1: March 1572

To Her Gracious Majesty from thine own true and loyal servant Gwen Glover.

Greetings and good health to thee. We pray for thy divine majesty at this time for we have heard rumour of great betrayal and the work of traitors in thy realm.

God Bless thee Elizabeth and know that we pray for thee each day and for the grace and wisdom of thy counsellors. Thy godchild Anne is well and strong in limb and humour. She is doted upon in this household but drives her loving nurse to distraction with her quick wit and wilful tongue. The tutor is schooling her well and following the commands that thou hast forwarded in thy missives. William is teaching her to ride a small Welsh cob and spends hours in the fields with her.

I Thank thee Elizabeth for thy great goodness to us all.

William and I wish thee to share our great joy. I am with child again and hope that with God's will I shall bring forth a brother or sister for Anne. We hope that you will share our happiness.

God Bless thee Your Grace.   *Gwen Glover*

Letter from Thomasina (The Queen's maidservant): March 1572

Greetings Dear Friend and congratulations on the news of thee being with child.

I write to thee because the Queen hath taken to her bed this last three days. Leicester and Burghley are keeping vigil at her side day and night. She screams and drags at her stomach complaining of ague. There was great alarm lest she be ill with poison but we that do know her best believe that the humours which beset her oft-time are running their course.

I impart all of this to thee since it was after receiving thy letter that she fell ill. The paper hath been tested by the alchemist for poison and dismissed as innocent, as is just and true.

I saw Her Majesty weeping and wailing when she read thy words, so beseech thee do not be alarmed if the Queen's wrath is upon thee for a while. I do not fear for Her Majesty's life as these tempers and fits of anger do take upon her. Have pity Gwen and understand. Her royal cousin Norfolk who hath been found guilty of treason hath sorely distressed her. She is in fear of signing for his death since he is of her own blood.

When the Queen is troubled by matters of State she doth take poorly matters of the heart. Your news hath hit her badly I fear, but thou art more privy to that than I.

I forward this to thee in secret Gwen, lest it fall into unworthy hands. Answer it not but await more news anon.

God spare our Blessed Queen Elizabeth that she might reign in truth and justice over her people.

Thomasina

Diary: 29th May 1572

We are blessed with twin boys! William is overjoyed and says they are lusty young fellows who will win the hearts of the ladies. In truth they are born too soon and are smaller than most. For my part I have survived the childbed and give thanks for that.

Diary: 1st July 1572

I have been weak this last two months and suffered the sweats and colic. The boys are well and have grown like their father. Sweet Jesus I am surrounded by red-haired firebrands! Anne is a dear kind little nurse who hath spoon-fed me broth on my sickbed.

William hath made contact with John Talbot again and

hath secured for him a position at the Wireworks at Tintern. His apprentice learning will serve him well it is said. News hath also come to us from John and Bethan, that Sarah Talbot hath returned to Bristol and hath been to visit them at the Dairy Farm.

Diary: 8th September 1572

William hath written to the Queen himself since we have heard not a word since my letter in March. It is unlike her to forget Anne's birthday and he feared for her health. I am not privy to the letter but assume he hath told her of the birth of our sons.

She responded by return of mail. He hath not shown me the letter but told me that she is well and wishes us all God speed. He says that Elizabeth endeavours to buy shares in the Wireworks herself and is pleased that William is standing by his word for the Talbot boy.

John Talbot arrived at Tintern last month and hath taken up his post. Bethan came with him and they are to marry in the spring. Mayhap she will get the sulky creature to smile!

Diary: 11th May 1573

We are preparing for John Talbot's wedding next week. William hath provided everything for the wedding breakfast and Bethan's dress is being made out of silk sent by the Queen, for we have more than Anne or I have need of.

Bethan is devoted to John; I know not why for he is neither goodly in manner nor feature. Still he barks at my William and it is only to please Bethan that he hath agreed to marry at the farm. I hope that he loves her, for she is a rare and lovely child.

The May blossom is like lace along the hedgerows already. I pray that the weather will keep fine for them, for the sea birds were circling the hills this morning.

We had a strange visitor two days since, when William was away at the Wireworks on business. 'Twas the bygone Mistress of Talbot Farm, Sarah, come in search of my William. She is as lovely as William hath told me and I was full glad he was away from the house. I fear she cometh after money or William or both. Now that she hath viewed the new farm buildings and the great farmhouse I believe she desireth it all.

We met as equals, she and I, both hath lived the life of a harlot and that of a respectable wife. She said that she would come again, but I, thinking fast, said no that she durst not come again and that if she wanted to contact William, then she must go to our agent in Tintern. She held my eyes in a challenging way but saw full well that she be no match for Gwen Glover!

Letter from Elizabeth to Gwen 30th September 1573

To Gwen, in whom we trust and with whom we have shared the secrets of our heart.

Thanks to thee for thy birthday gift and the embroidered kerchief from Anne Elizabeth, which I shall treasure above all the jewels in our royal crown.

Thy Queen hath reached the age of 40! Despite all the omens and speakers of doom, we have survived our enemies thus far and intend to lead the people on to greater glories.

I enclose for Anne a fan of white feathers with a handle of gold. It bears our lion emblem and the bear, which is the mark of Leicester. It was from his hand that I received the birthday gift and although we love him dearly, it doth not match the affection I bear for Anne Elizabeth.

Also, dear Gwen, our spies inform us that he hath secretly married the Douglas she-wolf. He shall suffer for that deceit in time, but for now we celebrate! Sweet Jesus be praised that we have married the people and not the man!

Gwen there is talk of plague in the west. Take care of the child with the nosegays we have sent for thee and sprinkle the wormwood in all thy bedding.

Bless thee all and praise be to God!

Elizabeth R

Diary: 23rd August 1575

Bethan Talbot came to visit today with news that she is with child again; her first child was stillborn just a twelvemonth after the wedding. She doth bring me great joy with her tales of the old Talbot Farm and the pouting

Mistress Sarah. The latter never did return to the farm after her visit, God be praised.

Bethan declares that Sarah met a German metal worker in Tintern and is kept by him at a grand lodging near to the Wireworks. She wants for nothing 'tis said, so I for one am content for her. William has never mentioned this so I suspect that he is ignorant of her being in the locality.

The boys run like young puppies around the farm and are into everything. William dotes on them and carries them one on each shoulder around the fields. They cause a terrible rumpus where're they find themselves and cook hath sworn to have them strapped if they get under her feet in the kitchen again. I love them with all my heart and yet they make me cry sometimes. Golden haired they might be but they both have a strong look of my first boy and I grieve for that dear little soul.

Anne Elizabeth hath grown tall like a fiery red lily. Her graceful carriage belies her wicked tongue for she doth speak oaths I have not used since I left the forest. William says that she hears it from the stable boys and mimics to be like them. She fell from her pony last Friday and would not eat her fish or rise from her bed all day. We sat at her side and I cried till my eye lids were puffed-up like ripe peaches. She hath recovered but I have forbidden William to let her ride in the meadow again.

The Queen writes to the child herself now and less often to me. She hath ruined her with trinkets and books. The royal progress was to Kenilworth this summer and the Queen reports it was magnificent. Thomasina doth give me news from time to time and hath been a good friend. Her tales of how the Queen doth sport with Leicester maketh me laugh.

I wonder what my life might have been if I had stayed at court or if William had not come and sought us out. 'Tis no use to fret about the stuff of dreams.

<u>Letter from Thomasina Autumn 1576</u>

Dearest Friend,

Greetings from this royal palace to thee and thy kin.

I have secured some French silk stockings for thee and put them with this letter – thou shalt be a lady out there in the devil's hills!

Our mistress talks less of Anne but hath shown me a sturdy oak chest, which she keeps hidden beneath her bed. Therein lie all the child's scribblings and such and she hath commanded me that if she be taken from this world then the chest must be sent to thee at the farm and given to Anne when she is of age.

The court is alive with rumours of the Master of the Horse and the Queen's cousin Lettice Knollys. There is talk of a secret marriage this time – I fear they will drive the Queen too far and then we shall all be made to pay!

I should be joyous if mayhap, at some time or place, we two could meet again. God's blessing be upon thee and the child. Thomasina.

<u>Letter from Queen Elizabeth to Gwen – 27th July 1577</u>

To My Dear Gwen who remains as always in our heart.

God bless thee all, thy Queen doth bid thee well.

Gwen, we are in fear of the plague and of it spreading to thy family. We shall not leave Greenwich this year for our usual progress. The Queen must protect herself for the sake of her people and the love they bear her.

Do not, therefore allow visitors or strangers to come to the farm until Winter's frosts can purge the evil vapours of the plague. We live in dread of those close to our heart being taken with the black boils of death.

Write directly and tell me how the children fare and also of William and thyself. The carrier of this letter hath been warned on pain of death, not to come within a furlong of the great house, but to despatch it to a servant at the gate.

My life remains as always in peril. The Pope hath now sanctioned my assassination and if the plague doth not run its course with me then some pox-ridden cleric will surely try to send this Prince to her maker.

We were right to send Anne Elizabeth with thee to safety Gwen.

Elizabeth R

<u>Diary: 25th January 1579</u>

William hath taken to his bed with the burning chest and sweating sickness. The boys are recovering from a bout of the same. Anne, Bethan and I have spent many a day brewing potions for them and for her husband who is also suffering from the sickness.

John Talbot is held in high esteem at the wireworks and hath made great progress there. Nearly 600 men are employed there making fishing hooks, rings, cages, lattices for windows and the like. The goods are exported to England and all over. William says that John and he are working well and that his heart is much eased now that they are easier in each other's company.

Bethan spends much time at the farm helping with Anne and the boys. She is still childless, having lost four babies. There was a visitor in these parts for her, come from the farm near Bristol where she once lived with John and Sarah. The farmer's widow hath died and all they own is to come to Bethan. She be a sweet-natured girl who doth deserve good fortune to my mind.

The Queen hath sent dogs for the boys; she says they are a rare breed of hunting dog. I am dismayed for the poor things were near dead on arrival and will likely give up the ghost within a week. I have never been able to abide her disregard for animal suffering. The whole of London rejoices in bear baiting and cock-fighting. The Queen herself took great amusement in it and therein did she and I differ, for I see no merriment in making poor creatures bleed. Perhaps that is why she is can play the queen and I could not.

She hath stopped sending so many letters to Anne. Methinks she is so much enamoured with her sea captains and the search for land and treasure that she hath put her friends in Wales from her mind. That is as it should be - for what hath we to do with the court and its jesters? We love her none the less and read avidly the news we receive from Thomasina.

Diary: 14th September 1579

The Queen hath written to William and talks seriously about the possibility of her marriage. He tells me that he knoweth not who she wants to marry most; the Duke d'Anjou who she names 'her pet frog' or 'her monkey' Jean de Simier who acts as an intermediary. My husband is much moved by this.

I'faith it breaketh my heart to know that still there is a bond between them. He doth not show me the contents of her letters to him and I declare I am sore troubled lest he be planning to go to her or some such adventure.

He doth mock me when I speak of such things. Last night when we did sport in our bed, he bade me not speak of the Queen when he was about his business serving his wife. He laughed, showing me his perfect white teeth and his twinkling eyes still youthful and wild. I would have pinched and swore at him, but I am changed since the boys and cannot jest with love like I used to. He is my husband and I am true to him. I do not jest as I once did.

As for the Queen she will not marry, trust in my word. I wish she would not trouble my William with such things. Mayhap she hopes that she still wields power over him.

There be no need for her to fret, for the Queen hath power over all men.

Chapter Thirty-Two

Gloriana

I leave here a gap of some ten years or more for it was private family time for me and William. We heard little from the Queen except for gifts for the children, especially books, so many that we are the only farmhouse in this part of Wales with a Library to match any great house in England. Books and portraits (mostly of the Queen), some sketches by Her Majesty and poetry written in her own hand.

She was determined to remain part of our lives and we have loved her for that. Twice or mayhap three times, she sent an artist from London to paint the children, mostly Anne of course, for she hath never seen the boys and there is not the attachment between them. The paintings and sketches were taken back to London, carefully wrapped in cloths to protect them until they reached the royal apartments. After the Queen's letter of September1579, there was a silence between us. William responded to her of course, but what passed between them in words I know not to this day. He would not speak of her proposed marriages to me.

These were glorious years for the Queen, a time in which her power and might were put to test. She was, as I knew she would be, triumphant in all things but those of the heart. I had word of it all from Thomasina, who still to this day I have never met again. The King of Spain's Armada was blown away and his treasures pirated time and time again. Elizabeth made a mockery of all those who tried to stand against her. Indeed her days and nights seem full of revelry and celebration.

Elizabeth cannot escape being human, however and she hath also suffered her share of pains. The death of Mary Queen of Scots hath cut her deep and I am told that she is tormented by nightmares about the Queen's lips moving after her head was struck from her neck. Such witchcraft doth not surprise me for that woman hath been surrounded by intrigue and murder. Her beloved Leicester died in 1588 and Thomasina said that her grief were like that of a child. She consoled herself with Essex and Raleigh and others but when there was news of William failing in health too, she was aghast. I would have gone to her but the days of my journeying to London are passed.

Bethan and Anne are like sisters. Bethan is not happily married I know but has her freedom since John Talbot spends so much time at the Wireworks. She is able to be part of our household when it suits her; which pleaseth me enough.

I discovered in 1585 that William hath been sending money every month to Sarah Talbot in Tintern. He swears to me on oath that they have not renewed their acquaintance and I believe him for I have kept him fulfilled in matters of the private sort. In 1588 she married her German wire-maker and hath left with him to make a home in Tenby. I am glad for her that she returned to Wales, for she would surely be dead of the French Pox by now if she had stayed working the new London Theatres.

Bethan and I took Anne to see the wedding at the church. Sarah Talbot is a beautiful woman. She came to speak to Bethan but seeing Anne Elizabeth cried out and kissed her cheeks tearfully. She fussed around the two of them and kept repeating how like her father Anne was and what she would have given for a daughter like her.

I grow too soft in my heart, for I felt sorrow for the woman. She was a lovely creature and as she bent towards Anne I was amazed at the soft plumpness of her skin and the fragrance that surrounded her like a floral haze. It filled my mind with memories of searing summer days when we strolled out of the forest shade to enjoy the sun's warmth. I remember the lavender and roses that had grown for years around the old Talbot farm. That was the fragrance that she carried and that suited her so well. I resolved that day to plant new bushes around the farm and true to my word I have.

Diary: 2nd March 1592

My William is dying. He fell from a horse last autumn, travelling on the road where the young monk turned over his cart some forty years since. William was not badly injured but the horse crushed his master's leg and he hath suffered the creeping blackness in it ever since. I have treated the open ulcers and rid the leg of poison, but it defies me and will not heal. He hath gradually weakened and this last month is spitting blood.

I have not been keeping my diary or writing letters much of late. Our lives have been busy and our emotions like swallows swooping and diving high and low as we live our lives through each other.

The boys work the farm and William hath done little other than the accounts this past five year. They are good boys and I know William is content that they will keep the farm and all he hath worked for. He still owns an interest in the Wireworks and is forever talking of plans for the place and its workers. I have scolded him for not writing all his ideas down, as I have learnt to do. He promises that one day he will. I fear he will not live to finish the job.

Diary: 14th March 1592

We have sat at his side this seven nights and more tears have been shed and prayers muttered than in all the years we have lived here. I did not leave him day or night. I watched him breathing slower and more gently until he slipped away. Just before the end he opened his eyes, the pupils now ringed with a fine grey border that made him look old and wise.

"Anne," he whispered to me "She must marry well and bring forth children."

"Sweet Jesus", thought I, "even on his death-bed he looks at me and speaks his daughter's name!" I bear shame for thinking that, for he read my thoughts.

Reader, he hath known the truth these many years and told me so.

"Dear Gwen, "he breathed, reaching for my hand "I love thee wife and I shall wait for thee. Remember that thou art my wife on earth and in heaven."

I kissed him and he breathed his last.

My husband died this day and I am cold with fear.

Diary: 16th March 1592

I buried my William this day and I yearn to follow him to the grave. My children are bereft. The farm is silent. I cannot write more.

Diary: 31st March 1592

Anne Elizabeth gave the Queen the news of her father's passing. She and Bethan have run the household since his death for I have no will to leave my bed let alone tend the farmhouse.

Anne came running to my bedroom this morning with news that the Queen hath sent a large consignment of furniture; confiscated from the homes of Lettuce Knollys after the death of her husband Leicester. The Queen hath been saving the goods for Anne and hopes that they will give her cheer at such a sad time.

As soon as I am fit I shall write to the Queen and say that the goods must be shared between Anne Elizabeth and the boys if we are to accept her generosity. I am not in fear of her, for nothing can touch me now I have lost my love.

Diary: 1st April 1592

All Fool's Day and this foolhardy woman hath risen from her bed and walked through the meadow to his grave in a vicious shower of rain. I hope to take a chill and be out of this grief by May.

Elizabeth concedes my wish about the furniture. She is in a state of high flux again over Raleigh's deceit with Bess Throckmorton. Know they not how the Queen doth hate a breach of trust? What good can come of these secret marriages and hidden births? Did they believe that the truth would not out? Now they needs must cool their passion in the Tower.

Does my clever, brave Elizabeth not see the irony in all of this?

Diary: 28th May 1592

I am not yet dead and have quitted my bed in anger at my

stupidity. Bethan tells me that Sarah Talbot was here with her husband and asked to put flowers on William's grave. They all grieve for him but none more than I.

Diary: 10th January 1593

Good news at last! Bethan is with child again and by God I shall use every potion I know to help her keep the child this time. How this miracle hath occurred I know not for she is rarely with her husband for more than a day or two at a time. He travels to Bristol and other ports with the wireworks trade and hath the arrogance of a peacock.

Bethan, poor dab, is sick every morning regular as the cockcrow. She is old to bear a child but her face and figure are like those of a young bride.

Diary: 1st June 1593

Plague hath scoured Bristol and come across the water to Chepstow. John Talbot is dead and ten more at the Wireworks are held up in their homes with it. Thanks be to God Bethan was with us and is safe thus far.

Diary: 5th June 1593

Praise be to God! Bethan hath delivered of a healthy boy. The child is born early, brought on by the shock of her husband's death I reckon. She cannot hide her joy which is unseemly so close after her husband's death.

We cannot help but be full of delight at the farm, for truth to tell the child is so bonny and strong. Fate do take a strange course sometimes, for indeed as I look into the child's face I see my own boys looking back at me. For reader, the boy hath a shock of bright red hair nothing like the dark looks of John Talbot.

I keep my own counsel but in my heart rejoice; for by God's grace Gwen Glover is surely now a grandmother!

Diary: 14th February 1594

Bethan and our son were married at Christmas and have moved to their own farm some three miles south of our home. There is a difference in age between them but it doth seem to matter not when thou art witness to their loving ways. She hath profited well from the sale of Burbage Farm and with my help they should prosper in their new abode.

Anne is melancholy since they left but will not hear of marriage herself. She states that someday she will travel the world and visit her Godmother in London. I tremble when she talks that way for fear of losing her. She maketh no real plans, however, and methinks the dreams are all in her head. There is no way a woman can do those things without a husband, unless thou art the Queen of course!

Diary: 14th April 1595

There are no elderflowers on the trees again this Spring, so there will be no wine made this year, other than parsnip and damson that is. That is how it hath been since William died; the trees that skirt the graveside will not blossom or fruit.

Anne do laugh at me but I swear it is because he is there waiting for me. I know he is there for I can feel him with me when I sit at his side in the meadow. I have planted flowers there too but none will grow. Bethan says the bees will not go to that part of the meadow because they seek out the lavender bushes at the other side of the farm. The roses too, on the south facing walls are full of blooms already; their fragrance fills the house with perfume.

One of the Morgan sons hath offered for Anne's hand in marriage. They are wealthy and powerful in these parts, but she will have none of it. I will not force her.

Letter from Queen Elizabeth to Gwen January 1596

To our dear friend and sister in Wales,

Greetings from your Queen and praise be to God for safe delivery from the old year into the new.

Forgive me Gwen for we write to thee in melancholy. We feel a great sadness this day and are in despair when we see those faithful ones around us growing weary with age.

Our dear Lord Burghley serves steadfastly as ever, but his knees are swollen and his face grimaces with pain when he doth stoop to kiss our hand. He took ill last month and we did feed him broth from the spoon. He hath recovered, praise Jesu, but will relapse anon we fear.

Our dear Anne Elizabeth, writes that she hath received several offers of marriage. It pleaseth me that she hath the power to enslave the hearts of men, as did her mother.

Gwen, advise her well I beseech thee. Bid her learn from the past of both women who she holds dear, for we have seen the deceit of men and held them dear in our hearts. Betwixt thee and this Queen the child will want for nought so must marry only for love if she choose to marry at all.

We are amazed and delighted that Anne hath befriended the child who stumbled upon us on board ship in Chepstow. How the Lord doth watch over those that honour him and brings them together in our sight!

God Bless thee Gwen.   *Elizabeth R*

Diary: 18th December 1598

William Cecil, Lord Burghley, died in August of this year and Anne received a long correspondence from the Queen, bewailing her loss and ranting against the passing of time. I have not received a note from her or Thomasina (who I fear might be ill or dead) since the last one I have shown to thee.

Sarah Talbot and her husband have been lost in a trading ship off the coast of Wales, whilst returning from a visit to his family in Germany. I feel the loss deeply although she was no friend of mine. I know so much of her story from Bethan and my William that I feel she is part of my story too. Something tells me however, that she will be safe and return one day. I do not wish her ill.

Anne hath rejected another suitor and bids me let her take over all the running of the household and the interest in the wireworks. In truth she declares she would be nowhere else and I am too old to make a fair job if it now. She were ever the blunt speaker, our Anne! She speaks the truth.

Both of our sons are married and have children. I am a grandmother to six in all and rejoice in their company. Bethan and my son are a loving couple and their cattle are amongst the finest in Wales.

Once more I am proud and content. Anne Elizabeth's old nurse is still at the farm with us and watched me writing my diary this eventide. She sayeth I was ever her best pupil, for without her patience I should never have learnt to read nor write. What a change hath come over this forest girl; I could never have dreamed of the life I was to enjoy.

How fate and the will of men do touch our lives and toss us on its sea of supremacy.

Herein my diary ends.   Gwen Glover   1604

Chapter Thirty-Three

Thy Will Be Done

Christmas 1602 brought improved strength and hope to those at the Talbot Farm and to the Queen at Whitehall. It seemed that although almost seventy years old, the Queen was able to overcome all ills and thus her court celebrated with renewed vigour.

Snow fell silently on Christmas Eve at the Talbot farm. Gwen sat at her fireside while Anne played the lute and sang a Welsh hymn softly. The family were all at the great farmhouse and the rooms were filled with happy childish voices. There was an air of expectancy, excitement and happiness.

The farm and estate were prospering and, under Anne's leadership, new proposals for the care of those working at the wireworks were being put in place. Taking forward her father's ideas, she had encouraged the workers to create a welfare scheme so that the aged or infirm received a pension. Compensation was paid to plague victims and their families and to the widows of wireworkers. Part of the profits of the company was put aside so that a Preacher could be given £8 a year to instruct employees in the Holy Scriptures. This was a philanthropic initiative almost without parallel in Wales at that time. It was a legacy that benefited many who depended on the Tintern works for a living. When Anne wrote of this to her Godmother, there was a tone of justice being done for the people of Tintern. She implied a great wrong being righted without ever daring to put that into words.

Elizabeth knew the history of Tintern Abbey and was aware of William's involvement. She knew that of course when she took an interest in its establishment and later when she bought shares in the company herself. Elizabeth craved the love of the people and wished to make amends. The Queen, however, would never have criticised her father's actions and made no comment upon the matter. In her heart she was glad, but her head was ruled by the divine right of kings.

In January Queen Elizabeth, after consulting her horoscope, moved to 'her warm winter box' that was Richmond Palace. But for a slight cold she was fit and well; despite a biting north-easterly wind and sudden drop in temperature. There was excitement as the queen prepared for a visit from the first ever envoy from Venice to be sent to England since Elizabeth had been on the throne. It was an important diplomatic occasion and The Queen was determined to appear well and in the prime of her life.

On 6th February Elizabeth Tudor held steady while an imperial crown was placed on her head. Her frail rheumatic body was dressed in silver and white taffeta edged with gold. The low-cut neckline was adorned with pearls and gemstones, which bedazzled the ambassador. Her make-up, heavier as each year made its mark on her striking features, could not mask the regal beauty with which she had always been blest. She spoke fluently in Italian and enchanted the court with her wit and humour, just as she had determined. She reigned supreme. It was to be her last public appearance.

Across the mountains of Wales a bleak wind blew up from the west and spiralled chaotically when it met the north-easterly blast. The forest arched its back and shuddered as the howling wind challenged the windbreak of woodland. Stone cold and deep with menace, the River Wye burst its banks.

Gwen took to her bed, complaining of 'a devil clawing at her bones' and a raw chest. The farmhouse tried to lie low but the relentless storm would not have it.

Anne Elizabeth mounted her horse and set out on a brief journey that should have taken but an hour. The stableman had tried to prevent her leaving, reluctantly handing her the reins. He looked up at the yellow-grey sky and sniffed at the damp air, like an animal seeking the scent of its prey.

"Must thee go out riding Miss Anne ? There is a storm brewing afore eventide."

Anne pulled her cloak around her shoulders and stretched leather gloves over her slender fingers and almost up to her elbows.

"Thank 'ee but have no fear" she replied confidently, "I shall return afore the Mistress is awake. Mayhap I should take the short-cut across the lowlands."

The blustery weather beat against the horse's flanks as he galloped towards the lower fields. Anne let her eyes squint but breathed deeply as the fresh air swept across the valley. She loved the land, the threat of winter and the wild beauty of the liberated horse. The errand was not essential but at times like this the farmhouse could get stuffy and smoky. William Glover's daughter needed fresh and open fields; she could not refuse a challenge from the elements.

The water table had been steadily rising throughout the autumn months due to consistently wet weather. Large stretches of the valley were waterlogged but it was not discernible from a distance. The first sign of danger was the stink of a rotting corpse, which hit the back of her throat with a sickly-sweet stench. Alarmed, she reined in the horse fiercely and glanced anxiously around her. Some poor creature had met its end in a grisly way, trapped in the deep sticky mud, which had coated its hide and dragged it down into the morass.

Its yellow eyes were wide and staring in shocked amazement at the catastrophe that had brought its demise. Its tongue lolled, obscenely black, from the side of its jaw. Nausea surged through Anne and she turned swiftly away from the scene expecting to vomit. Her horse, panic-stricken by the clinging sludge around its hooves and the overpowering stink of death, jolted forward and reared up with a terrified neigh.

Her balance lost, Anne was flung from the horse and into the mire. She was winded for a few minutes only and thought at first she had survived the fall quite well. It was only when she tried to lift her legs and struggled to free herself that she felt the searing pain in her left leg and saw blood pumping into grotesque scarlet pools on the surface of the mud. Almost at once the scowling black clouds that had hung motionless, spectators at this gruesome cull, let fall the bitter rain.

Anne's "breakaway rides", as she called them, usually lasted an hour at the most. When she did not return after two hours her brother and two farm workers set off to find her. Despite appalling conditions and a truly gruesome scene when they found her, they rescued Anne. She was brought back to her home suffering from shock, loss of blood and exposure to the freezing elements. Her left leg had been crushed. For two long days she lay unconscious; her life ebbing away. Gwen was reminded of Elizabeth's leg injury and rapidly applied the same poultices and ointments which had worked before. It was to little avail, however, for too much blood had soaked back into the Welsh soil. The Queen had to be informed of the accident and the sombre news of her God-daughter's grave illness. It was made clear that Anne Elizabeth was not expected to survive the fall.

It was the middle of February 1603. When the messenger brought the news to Richmond, the Queen had just left the deathbed of her cousin and close friend, the Countess of Nottingham. On almost the same day, her coronation ring had to be sawn from her finger. That great symbol of power, which of late had cut so deeply into Elizabeth's swollen finger, had been forcibly removed. For Elizabeth it was like removing her wedding ring, for this had been a marriage between a monarch and her people. Elizabeth gave in to a deep despair from which she could not recover.

"Bad news, gravely ill….." murmured the Queen, "We are done with these sorrows. Dear Kat, sweet Robert, Essex, Lord Burghley….all gone."

There seemed no longer a reason to live and in facing that, the Queen submitted to her fate.

Elizabeth Tudor had a cold, which turned to bronchitis. Foul swellings and ulcers lined her throat and she could not be tempted to eat. She withdrew to the Privy Chamber and sat on cushions for hours on end; staring, remembering and grieving. Those around her despaired of how to help the Queen:

"Her majesty doth sit for hours on end without speaking or seeming to know that we are with her. She looks from this world into the mysteries beyond and all the time sucks at her finger like a frightened child."

If any of those present had dared to venture closer to Elizabeth Tudor, they might have observed that it was not her finger she sucked, but a cross. Clutched in her hand was The David Cross that William Glover had given her so many years before. She kissed it, held it close to her lips and prayed that the end would come quickly and that she might be free from all earthly restraints at last. Her mind was full of images; the faces she had not seen for many years, the child she had sent to Wales but whom she longed to be with, William Glover, Gwen and all those who belonged in her secret world where she was a woman and not a Queen.

The Privy chamber was fetid with the soiled clothing and cushions of the Queen. Her perfumes and spices could not hide the rank odour of a body that was becoming diseased by neglect, as the days melted away. Elizabeth was not suffering from a fatal illness other than her wish to give up the ghost. She was, as ever, in terror of the hand of death but could no longer endure the pain of grief. Eventually she was persuaded to stand, which she did for fifteen hours, but still she would not rest in her bed or take food. The most important men in the land gathered to wait for the Queen's demise. Already preparations were in place to send messengers north to Scotland, where James, son of Mary Queen of Scots, awaited the call to power. There was little discretion as Elizabeth's condition deteriorated; the question of the succession was the main concern, as the Queen knew it would be.

The courtiers and ladies of the chamber were finally

allowed to help her to the high wooden bed. As she was raised up she caught Robert Cecil's pitying expression. She held his eye for a moment and then stabbed with an emaciated finger, indicating something underneath her great bed. He returned her action immediately by nodding his head and she was relieved, knowing him to be in this last secret act, a true son of his loyal father. Just as Elizabeth had feared, once she had taken to her bed, the end was upon her. An abscess burst in her gullet, which at first gave some relief. A little rosewater was dribbled between her lips. Then the throat and chest condition worsened until she lost the power of speech. She was glad of it; for then she could not betray her Tudor blood and declare a Stuart King to be her successor.

Evening brushed aside the grey March day and spread itself comfortingly across Richmond Palace. The Queen let herself glide into the gentle waters of a timeless sleep. There was little left to fear; for in the peaceful depths of oblivion there were many old friends awaiting her passing. Her head rested on a silken pillow; the embroidered sheet embraced her wasted frame as the silence finally caressed her. Doctor Parry, her favourite chaplain, had been watching over her and praying for her departed soul. As he indicated that she was dead, the rain suddenly spattered against the leaded window protesting in disbelief that this could have ended at last. It was almost three o'clock on Thursday morning, 24th March 1603.

Almost at once, according to agreed arrangements, Lady Scrope gently eased a sapphire ring from the dead Queen's finger. As she did so the Queen's palm unfurled and from it The David Cross fell noiselessly to the floor. At once Robert Cecil stooped to retrieve it and secreted it away safely. No one noticed this swift action, as all eyes in the room followed Lady Scope and the sapphire ring. She crossed to the window and looked for the face of her brother Robert Carey. Already saddled and ready to ride North, Carey caught the ring as it was tossed down towards him. As the rain began to fall steadily in an unrepentant show of grief, he clattered out of the courtyard and headed for Scotland and James Stuart.

Chapter Thirty-Four

Of Lavender and Rose

April has always been the most unsettling month; stirring passions, taking away and giving in a headstrong arrogant way. When Robert Cecil's special messenger arrived, bad-tempered and truculent, at the Glover farm, he was welcomed with some restraint. Gwen was still in mourning and thought that her communication with the English court had finally ended with the Queen's passing.

He brought with him a heavy gilt-trimmed box that had been hidden in the Queen's Privy Chamber for many years. She had slept many nights with it by her side for it symbolised the private world in which Anne Elizabeth, Gwen and William Glover were always key players. Thomasina was the only one who knew of it for many years, but after her departure, Lord Burghley and then his son were told of its existence and where it should be sent on the Queen's death. The Queen's instructions were followed precisely.

The box was for Gwen but most of the contents, she soon discovered, were to be passed on to Anne. The box of course also contained The David Cross which was returned at last to Wales. Gwen was shocked, intrigued and a little in fear of unwrapping the cross and holding it. This ancient cross had been the centre of religious conviction, passionate protection and a cause of suffering and death in the past. For Gwen the cross had been crucial to her finding William and impacted upon the lives of others they knew. Gwen wondered how many past and future lives might be enriched or destroyed by its power. The next destination of this precious religious artefact was something to be discussed and decided over time; too important a decision to be left to the Glover family alone. For now, Gwen placed it carefully back in the box. She was not yet ready to tell her family what history she knew of the cross or why it was passed to her for safekeeping.

It was an odd combination of gifts that the Queen had willed to Gwen:

A bag of fine muslin filled with dried lavender heads ("For we know that thou art enamoured of the fragrance and use the plant in thy healing receipts") a pot pourri of rose petals and a phial of rose perfume ("From our gardens at Hampton Court where we were so happy"), a brooch of diamonds and rubies fashioned in the Tudor Rose, a pair of lavender calf-skin gloves once belonging to Elizabeth ("For thou did remark on their loveliness"), a lace baby's bonnet ("Placed on Anne Elizabeth's dear head straightway after she arrived in this world") and a string of pearls ("For thee Gwen, that come what may thou shalt never be poor or want for ought").

There were substantial bequests of gold and fine brocades, leather and velvet for the boys and their families. The materials were wrapped in protective fleece and strapped to the rider's horse. It was Anne, however, who received the true bounty of the Queen's favours for the box was heavy with priceless gifts for her.

It was a private collection or rare and beautiful gems fashioned into all manner of designs. Some were the gifts from one royal hand to another; others were the booty from sea captains' voyages. Gwen held them and let her imagination run free; the treasures from far off lands, long salted by the oceans and forged by the fire of island sunshine. It was a world unknown to Gwen and her kindred.

Also in the box there was a letter and it was this that was meant as the greatest gift for Anne Elizabeth. The contents of the letter were explosive and as Anne still lay so poorly, Gwen presumed to read the letter first herself and then decide upon who should read it after her.

She was the only remaining conspirator and she inherited the power to act as she alone thought fit.

My Dear heart Anne Elizabeth,

Who rejoiceth in our Mother's name, our own name and that of our grandmother Elizabeth of York.

It is my intention that this queen shall have passed to eternal rest when thou discovereth this letter. However, that may not be so, for we have long since ceased to fight against the workings of fate.

Sweet child, first I give thee my greeting and my blessing and pray that thou shalt have a goodly and favoured life.

Thy father William hath loved thee as he should and Gwen hath, we know, loved and cared for thee in all things. That is as it should be and as we have planned.

There may perchance, have been times when thou hast wondered what thy family in Wales hath done to deserve the favours of a Tudor Queen. Thou must know by now that my grandfather Henry Tudor was born in Pembroke Castle and it was an army of Welshmen that carried him to London and made him the first Tudor king. Always remember with pride thy Welsh heritage sweet Anne Elizabeth, as we have done here in London.

Gwen hath told thee all oft times of my journey to Wales and of how providence willed that my life be saved by William and Gwen. That would be reason enough for thee all to have our blessing and support. That visit, in truth was of great moment for this Prince, for therein I have learnt to love and to cherish the gift of freedom.

Anne, this royal Elizabeth hath never known the true freedom that is thy right. Born into the seat of power, I have carried the burden and blessing of royal blood alone. I am fortunate indeed to have survived the early years but cannot forget how torture and death have courted this royal daughter.

My life hath been a catalogue of threats, plots, intrigue and all the time there is a cloud of conspiracy hovering around the crown. Some of those I have loved deceived and lied for their own ends. They sought to stand for a while in the sun with their prince. Foreigners and cousins have tried to have this Queen killed and still I am in daily fear of my life. Think on this when thou read onwards and be advised that our intentions were always for thy good.

My love for thy Father William Glover hath been deeper than thou could have guessed. He hath been so like a kindred spirit unto this Queen and understanding of her heart, that we were as one in our affection. Had he claimed to be our kinsman we could not have denied it.

As the fates willed he became my lover and thou our blessed child.

I returned to London, having tasted freedom for a brief period. I'faith I also discovered that my enemies seek me out where're I hide and that life is easily traded for a crown.

On my return to power in England, I found myself to be with child. The joyous secret blazed in my heart and I resolved to defy the world and bring the child forth as the royal successor. I sent for Gwen, whose own tragedy still haunted her and who had become our trusted friend. Willingly she came to court and for months we shared great happiness, as the babe grew strong in my womb. We needed each other and we shared the months of waiting.

Elizabeth the woman became powerless against the might of Elizabeth the Queen, for as the child was growing, all around the dangers grew. We bore witness to the plight of the Scottish Queen, my cousin Mary. As the unborn child stirred, we watched that cousin lose her crown and the babe be taken from her.

Should I risk the stability of the throne and the love of the people for the sake of my own selfish heart? Dare I risk a child's life as well as my own?

Should I let my heart rule the Queen and condemn thee to a life that is never thine own?

When William came in search of his Queen I saw the working of destiny and the chance to give thee thy freedom. In Gwen and William, thy true blood father, there was an opportunity for thee to live a full life and marry for love.

Anne, I have denied thee thy royal birthright but given to thee the power of freedom.

It is for thee now to decide what thou wouldst wish, for this letter can be the evidence of thy succession if that is thy will. Make no mistake that thy Queen takes great pride in her right to rule her people and would not have betrayed her birthright and destiny. My life carries the pleasures and burden of kingship and that is the Lord's doing. I am the happiest of women to do His will for it hath been a marvellous duty in our eyes. Thou must make thine own peace with God now and decide upon thy future.

Know that I have been thy Queen and thy Godmother but in my heart thou hast always been my beloved child.

God Bless thee Anne Elizabeth.   God keep thee safe, my daughter.

Elizabeth R   *29th May 1602*

Gwen read and re-read the words, holding a magnifier to her failing eyes. She allowed the tears to fall and find their way through the lines that lovingly traced the years upon her face. Her hair, still long and mostly brown, was plaited and coiled under a soft woollen bonnet. As the memories crowded in upon her, she felt young again. She stretched up slowly and took the bonnet from her head. Her fingers, gnarled and arthritic, fumbled with the pins that held the plaits. They tumbled down heavily across her shoulders. She let them loose so that she could feel again the long wavy hair across her breast and back, billowing as it used to when she was strong and young.

They had concealed the truth so well, that she had come to believe it herself. The months of padding out her belly and feigning the ills of pregnancy, while the Queen secretly loosened her stays, brought memories back which filled Gwen with delight.

The child, born so easily, had been an innocent supporter of the plot. The midwife who assisted them had been paid handsomely but died shortly after the birth and so posed no threat to the conspiracy. Anne herself had caused no problems for her royal mother and had bonded readily with Gwen, to the dismay oft times, of the Queen. Sending the child from court had been an heroic and unthinkably painful decision for Elizabeth to make. Gwen had prepared herself for the possibility that at any time the Queen might change her mind and not be able to keep away from her daughter.

The reappearance of William Glover was a double heartbreak for the Queen. It also seemed to Elizabeth to be a sign as to what she must do. They were made from a strong united mould, Gwen and her Queen. Together with William Glover, who of all of them seemed to find this the hardest to bear, they had acted out of love for the child and each other.

Gwen slowly pulled herself out of the fireside chair that had been her comfort and confidant during the anxious hours following Anne's accident. For now, only Gwen and the letter in her hand bore witness to this story. It revealed the conspiracy of a Tudor Queen and the birth right of Anne Elizabeth Glover. It was potentially life-threatening for Anne but dazzling in its possibilities as the heir to the throne. Revealing the truth would probably incur violence, intrigue and death for innocent lives caught up in the dispute. The authenticity of the letter would be questioned. It could be a fatal mistake for the whole family and many other innocents. Gazing into the comforting flames of the farmhouse hearth, it would have been easy to let the fire consume the frightening implications of the letter. In a few moments the secrets it betrayed could be destroyed forever. The family would live without fear, safe in their ignorance.

"Damn you Elizabeth Tudor" murmured Gwen "You are still in control of our lives and breaking my heart!"

Angry bitter tears stung Gwen's eyes. Trembling with emotion she climbed the stone stairs leading to the chamber where Anne Elizabeth lay, still in recovery and very weak. Despite all the damage and illness following her accident, she lived on. Weak after months of pain, she opened her eyes and welcomed Gwen. She smiled knowing that her recovery was due only to the loving care and healing knowledge of Gwen Glover. Anne's life was not out of danger; she would seem to recover almost completely and then faulter and slip back into exhaustion and pain.

Should Gwen now renounce the title of Mother to this dear girl? What would happen when Anne realised that her true birth mother was of royal blood? How would she respond to lies and deceit however well-meaning? How would the rest of the family respond to the news?

This was a burden that Gwen felt heavily and she wished, as she so often did, that her husband was still alive to share it with her.

Gwen entered the room softly and kissed Anne's pale cheek.

"I have a letter for you my love; a letter from London." She spoke in a whisper but Anne's eyes opened wide and they shone with excitement. She had been told of the Queen's death and been saddened but had not grieved.

"Is it from the Queen?" Anne asked.

"Yes it is," Gwen replied, "and it is quite important."

Anne knew of the friendship between her parents and the Queen but had never really questioned it.

"Thank you mother." Anne murmured. As she spoke her eyes closed and smiling she relaxed into a contented sleep.

Gwen renamed the Talbot farm in 1604, declaring that the land belonged to her family and that her husband had repaid his debt to the Talbots. It is a quiet land now with long buried secrets that only whisper to themselves when the warm winds blow from the west.

The Glover graves are gone, deeply submerged in the Welsh meadow and part of the very soil on which their sleepers walked. The rose bushes have been allowed to run wild and free, their Tudor red petals bleached by the sun of a thousand days. The lavender grew woody with age and finally decayed, as is the way of all things.

On summer evenings, especially in May, you might wish to wander in the meadow there and listen for the murmurings lost in time. There is a gentle breeze which seems to travel from the west, bringing with it a soft hum and a delicate scent. It is the gift of Sarah Talbot as she returns to join the spirits there, it is the loving tribute of Gwen and the secrets of a Queen.

It is how you will know them and that they live on in peace; it is the scent of lavender and rose.

Printed in Great Britain
by Amazon